D0923467

ALL MEN ARE MAD

*by Philippe Thoby-Marcelin
and Pierre Marcelin*

CANAPÉ VERT
THE BEAST OF THE HAITIAN HILLS
THE PENCIL OF GOD
ALL MEN ARE MAD

ALL MEN ARE MAD

Philippe Thoby-Marcelin
and
Pierre Marcelin

with an Introduction by
Edmund Wilson

translated from the French by
Eva Thoby-Marcelin

FARRAR, STRAUS & GIROUX
New York

Introduction

Sometime in 1944, when I was regularly reviewing books for the *New Yorker,* there fell into my hands a translation of a novel called *Canapé Vert,* by two brothers, Philippe Thoby-Marcelin and Pierre Marcelin, which had just won a prize, as the candidate from Haiti, in a Latin American fiction contest. This book seemed to me very strange, quite unlike any piece of fiction that I had ever seen, and it piqued my curiosity. It was so evident that the translation was unreliable that I applied to the publisher for the original French, and this partly cleared up the mystery, for the translator had actually tampered with the text, and his French was so inadequate that he had sometimes mistaken the meanings of common enough words and phrases. But the story was still queer and confusing. I knew nothing about vodou then and did not know that one of its principal features was the possession of its worshippers by the vodou deities. These deities, though they vary in different localities, sometimes retain their personalities through many generations, and the possessed who impersonate them display the same characteristics. The possessed man or woman assumes the name and takes over the voice and the nature and habits of the *loa* by whom he is "mounted." He has to be deferred to by others, and his inclinations have to be indulged as if he were actually this deity. The sinister Baron Samedi, who, though sensual and ribald, presides over cemeteries, likes to wear a top hat and dark glasses, and always speaks in a nasal voice. When, in the Marcelins' *La Bête de Museau,* he has "mounted" an oppressed servant girl, he is found at his ease in the kitchen, smoking the cigars and drinking the rum which are his personal perquisites. In their latest novel, the ogress Marinette Braschèche can terrify her Estinval, even though he is supposed to be an adept at sorcery, when she has gained possession of his wife.

This strange situation itself provides many materials for drama, once the reader has grasped the fact that the characters have double roles—that, on the one hand, they are real people with the normal kind of personal relations with others while, on the other, they are living in an imaginary world of vodou mythology and magic. But the two brothers who write these books are well-educated and highly intelligent natives of Port-au-Prince, with a training in French culture behind their vodou lore, who have known how to present their characters in an anthropological perspective that extends beyond the special customs of Haiti, and who are aware of the power of mythologies in all the doings of the human race even in countries which are supposed to be more or less enlightened. The Soviet secret police used to think of themselves as embodying the Sword of the Proletariat; the members of the Ku Klux Klan, when they put on white hoods and robes, could play the parts of Wizards and Kleagles who were at liberty to hunt and lynch Negroes, while the average American citizen could always identify himself with a benevolent bearded Uncle Sam, who rights wrongs in an old-fashioned tall hat. It is partly the fascination of these unusual stories themselves but also, I think, partly their universal application that has made such apparently very regional productions so surprisingly successful in English. The second of the Marcelins' novels, *La Bête de Musseau (The Beast of the Haitian Hills)*, of 1946, had a sale of over 80,000 in the Reading Program of *Time* magazine; and there was some question of turning the third, *Le Crayon de Dieu (The Pencil of God)*, 1951, into an American musical show.

But the brothers, who had always worked together, were now to be condemned to an enforced separation. M. Philippe Thoby-Marcelin came to work in the Pan American Union in Washington and married an American wife, while his brother remained in Haiti. Eventually the two collaborators effected a partial rapprochement. Pierre arranges to spend his summers in the United States with Philippe, and they have now written another novel, which seems to me, to date, their masterpiece. It is in some ways rather different from its predecessors. It covers a good deal more ground, involving a greater variety of social types, and its tone is somewhat different. The earlier novels of the Marcelins had something of the fresh excitement of the relatively recent discovery by sophisticated city-dwellers, brought up in the Catholic religion and the tradition of French culture, of the more or less fantastic life in a kind of visionary world of the African denizens of the hinterland. Their new novel, *Tous les Hommes Sont Fous (All Men Are Mad)*, is drier and more objective. It is based on, though it does not follow literally, a real episode in Haitian history. In 1942, there was a special effort on the part of the Catholic Church to redeem the vodou worshippers for Christianity. These Catholic priests had long acquiesced in a conveniently stabilized form of what is known theologically as syncretism—that is, the less advanced Haitians practised a double cult, and for the figures in the Christian hierarchy set up altars which included also a hierarchy of vodou opposite numbers. Thus, reigning with the Virgin Mary, stood the by no means virgin goddess of love called Erzilie; the warrior Ogou Ferraille, who figures in the present novel, was identified with St. James; Papa Legba, who presides over journeys, was paired with St. Anthony; and St. Patrick, with his foot on a snake, was paired with Dumballa, the snake deity. I was once in Haiti near Christmas and found that the Christmas cards, along with "Joyeux Noël," were sometimes decorated with a snake that represented the last of these *loas*.

But now, contrary to recent custom, the Church made an attempt to abolish all this. It obtained from the President of Haiti a circular letter to the local prefects directing them to coöperate in the campaign against vodou. The Marcelins have dramatized this campaign as conducted, in the town of Boischandelle, by a newly arrived young French priest, Père le Bellec. He has mobilized to assist him a band of young Catholic zealots who call themselves the Soldiers of St. Michael. This results in a disastrous mess. A clever and sly old "doctor" has been trying to play it both ways, to pass as supporting both *papa Bon Dieu* and the vodou *loas* or *mystères,* but many of the backwoods natives of the "commune" where the story takes place are contemptuous of the *petit monpère* reformer and turn out against the Soldiers of St.

Michael, who have been burning the images of the *loas,* and in the confusion a vodou temple is also burnt. Both sides make a ludicrous showing, and the Catholics accomplish nothing lasting. A young boy, brought up in vodou, believes himself to be possessed by the formidable Ogou Ferraille, the *loa* of war and fire, and he stands at the head of the resistance. He is arrested and put in prison, still defying the civil authorities, and he dies as the result of a beating, in consequence of his inability to resign his supernatural authority.

This episode is one of the climaxes of the story, but it is embedded in a narrative much more complicated than those of the other books of the Marcelins. One new element that here appears is the world of provincial officialdom, with its pretentious and grotesque jargon, in which the petty political intrigues and the rather sordid fornications are discussed in a stilted formal language, studded with Latin tags. (It is to be hoped that the opening conversation between the Judge, the Lieutenant and the Mayor, which constitutes an exposition of the fundamental situation, will not discourage the reader from following the later developments of the issues here partly veiled.) We have also the younger generation, delinquent and sometimes criminal, and the life of the taverns and brothels to which the officials resort. All this is presented by the Marcelins in a style of unemphasized irony that belongs to the French tradition of Maupassant and Anatole France. There is almost no overt comment; the criticism is all implied. And though what happens, if viewed in an ironic light, is often extremely funny, what is suggested is also pathetic. It is sad that human beings should be living with such delusions and in such limitations; should be talking such inflated nonsense, suffering helplessly from such wretched diseases, be intimidated and dominated by such outlandish superstitions. The vodouists and the Roman Catholics are equally inept and mistaken. Here again the special plight of the Haitians is made to extend a perspective to the miseries and the futilities of the whole human race, to our bitter "ideological" conflicts and our apparently pointless ambitions. *All Men Are Mad* is a very entertaining but also a troubling book, and it is a most distinguished work of literature.

Edmund Wilson

ALL MEN ARE MAD

Folly speaks

Whatever opinion the world holds of me (for I am well aware what a bad name I have even among the greatest fools), it is none the less true that I, and I alone, have the power to bring cheer to the hearts of gods and men.

. . . I hold sway over the whole universe and exert my rule even over kings.

ERASMUS, *In Praise of Folly*

I

At Boischandelle—a village of some three thousand souls, located somewhere in the mountains of the West— the quarrel of the *Rejetés* exploded on a clear, dry day, one of those provincial Sundays conducive to the *dolce far niente* of the *cabicha* rather than the active life of religious wars.

That day, Macdonald Origène, then Mayor of the commune, was celebrating his forty-second birthday. He had invited to lunch only the highest officials, Lieutenant Bellami and the Justice of the Peace, Septimus Morency, who represented with him the order established by the grace of God in the Republic of Haiti.

It was June, nearing the solstice, and though the house was exposed to the wind from the lakes, whose sheets of quicksilver shone in the sun—for Boischandelle clusters on top of a round hill to the northeast of the La Selle range, its houses blackened by the harsh weather and topped with corrugated tin roofs—it was getting warm inside. Hence, Madame Origène, provident hostess, had set the table in the courtyard in the fragrant shade of a curtain of pine trees, so the guests were not uncomfortable.

5

As the meal was nearing its end, Macdonald Origène suddenly felt his tongue loosen with an unusual suppleness and felicity. He was a real man, as they say in our country, tall and broad-shouldered, with a sparse little mustache, who was methodically building himself the career of a man of substance, one of those thoughtful, perspicacious men who, in order to be considered wise, force themselves to be reserved and are stingy with their smile.

Of course, having copiously celebrated his birthday since the day before, he was somewhat excited. But also, he had just recalled the strong sermon on superstition which the new parish priest had given at High Mass, a veritable diatribe in which, promising to root out vodou from the region of Boischandelle—a task which surely was the responsibility of his noble ministry—he had been carried away to the point of saying that he would do it without putting on kid gloves ("by force even, if necessary, my very dear brethren"), and worse still, he had claimed the unconditional support of the President of the Republic.

At the moment, of course, Macdonald Origène had pricked up his ears, smelling, like a good watchdog, that it was but a straw in the wind pregnant with implications, but his brain, then clouded from the heavy sleep that follows a drinking bout, couldn't concentrate on a specific accusation. Now that additional drinks were dissipating the fog of the previous celebration, for he had prudently kept count "with the pertinent sagacity of the Graduate Therapeutist," as Septimus Morency, champion of "fine speech" had learnedly remarked, a brilliant idea was beginning to dawn in his head. "What!" he exclaimed to himself. "He comes. . . . He tells us. . . . Then, who am I?" Acutely conscious of his municipal responsibilities, Macdonald Origène vigorously wiped his mouth, still full of rice, mushrooms, and peas.

"Father Le Bellec, you see . . . ," he said as he chewed, "that little priest . . . uh . . . uh . . . let me tell you . . . once for all, my friends . . . what I think of him!" With a decisive male fist he put his napkin down on the table. "You can believe me or not, gentlemen . . . the fact is he's an intriguer . . . a con . . . spirator!"

Having spoken, then swallowed his last mouthful, he took a deep breath, loosened his belt, and patted his stomach, whose imposing roundness, in his opinion, attested to an honestly-come-by prosperity—for he had done everything to deserve it. (He had even set about it a long time before. Once, when he was a junior at the Lycée Pétion, he had had published in the Port-au-Prince newspapers this majestic notice: "We ask the public in general and our friends in particular to be advised that, for important personal reasons, we wish no longer to be called by the nickname Gègène. Those who wish to show us their cordiality in a special way may henceforth call us Mac.") And now this young father, a little priest . . . a greenhorn, to sum it up . . . no, but . . . who does he think he is, that one?

With a nervous gesture, Macdonald Origène crossed his knife and fork on his plate and continued: "For, after all, gentlemen, if the President of the Republic, our incomparable and beloved Chief . . . and you know as well as I do, don't you, that he's a reasonable man, an eminent politician . . . and no one is unaware, besides, that he has long been preoccupied with this annoying problem, has he not? . . . uh . . . uh . . . that he has scrutinized it in all its depth . . . for, in short, it's not for nothing that he was a seminarist in his youth . . . if then, in order that we may more worthily occupy the place which is rightly ours in the harmonious concert of the civilized nations of the planet . . . if the Chief, I say, desires to free our towns and countryside from the old beliefs of ancestral Africa . . . uh . . . uh . . . do you think he'll ever do it *manu militari,* as this stranger in a cassock claims? . . . You realize . . . a man, you see, who means to manage the interests of the Haitian community with the equitable care of a good paterfamilias . . . don't you see . . . uh . . . uh . . . After all, my friends, tell me frankly and loyally!"

"Very strong, that!" loudly proclaimed Septimus Morency, adjusting his pince-nez of smoked glass. "Ver-ry strong! But also very debatable. . . . And, first of all, my dear Mac, an interlocutory question. The Presidency . . . or rather, as you have specifically defined it: the Chief . . . that paladin of the noble civilizing concerns of the nationality, not to say, the Hamitic race in its perfect totality, did he not initial with his golden pen an administrative dispatch of circular trajectory in which he instructed roundly, and even squarely, the illustrious prefects of the transcendent and ascensionist Republic of Haiti that it was their duty to lend aid and assistance to the sacrosanct clergy in its congruent socio-logico-religious and anti-paganistic proceedings?"

Although he was thin and looked weak, the Justice of the Peace was seething from the heat of tropical eloquence that gushed spontaneously from his mouth, enamored as it was of bombastic neologisms, with not the faintest concern for the correctness of the terms or the aptness of the Latin quotations; his barren flesh,

8

which he clothed all year round in white trousers and a black alpaca jacket, exuded an acrid dampness that steamed his glasses. He took them off his thin, slightly retroussé nose and solemnly wiped them with an enormous red snufftaker's handkerchief, and then blotted his face, whose bronze tone heightened at the cheeks to a light copper tint. Still, he was not tired. He felt quite at ease, very happy to give vent to that systematic verbalism with the intemperate flow he called "fine speech" and which he fed from the most diverse sources: dictionaries, textbooks of law and philosophy, great orators of the pulpit and bar, and especially the stern representatives of our "young Haitian science," whose aggressive and highly specialized secret vocabulary transported him to the purest heights of poetic gratuitousness.

"Granted, Justice Sèpe, granted!" said Macdonald Origène.

But since he was hardly trained for contests in eloquence and was searching for words to reply, Lieutenant Bellami, who quite simply admired the Justice of the Peace's language, took advantage of the opportunity to express his feeling.

"Sèpe, dear friend," he said enthusiastically, "you are decidedly an extraordinary man, a child of the Good Lord, who made you with his own hands. As for speaking with elegance, you beat everybody. And may thunder strike me, such French! Where in the world did you learn to make it paw the ground like that?"

"In the modest dwelling of my family ancestry and from no living soul!" he trumpeted, proud of his self-education but stopping short of confessing that the untimely death of Morency senior, clerk of the civil court of Les Cayes, had forced him to stop his classic

9

studies when he was just beginning his freshman year in high school. "I am an anthumous son of my works. My elocutive and dialectic faculties have been refined, *mutatis mutandis,* by daily and persistent contact with immortal rhetors, classic as well as romantic, all of them departed in the ancient or modern era. For, as stated in the maximal adage in the pink pages of the illustrated *Petit Larousse,* if not in the peremptory garden of the Graeco-Latin roots, *asinus asinum fricat.* Hence, my noble Centurion, we are polished."

"Point of order!" the Mayor of Boischandelle uttered haughtily and somewhat ironically. He had just put together the principal elements of his argumentation.

"Of course, Mayor Origène!" protested the Justice of the Peace, courteously aggressive. "Of course! It is surely your turn to have the floor. So it is willed by the impartial custom that democratically governs the allotment of time within the protocol-prone deliberative assemblies. As for Lieutenant Bellami and your humble servant . . . " He bowed low, with his hand on his heart. "We are only trying in our soul and conscience to fill for the moment the temporary void created by your strategic retreat into the high metaphysical spheres of Socratic meditation."

Macdonald Origène gave him a faint smile. "As I just told you, Justice Sèpe . . . and no one can contradict me on this fundamental point . . . uh . . . uh . . . you, least of all, I am happy to acknowledge . . . His Excellency the President of the Republic is a statesman in the fullest meaning of the word . . . a contemporary Marcus Aurelius, I dare say . . . you see, don't you see? . . . an eminent sage whose Promethean stature . . . you realize . . . tops the average man by a thousand cubits!"

"Very sound, dear friend, ve-ry sound! So, taking into account the executive wisdom of the Chief, with all commensurate veneration, I'll go several milestones beyond your kilometric though vertical evaluation concerning the presidential merits. I will say . . . and what, great God, could one not say in praise of them, since a single curved genuflection is enough to glean abundantly in the apologetic fields of glorious reminiscences? . . . I'll say, therefore, that he is, in the last analysis, a spiritualist if not consubstantial son of the implicit mother of the Gracchi."

"So, Justice Sèpe, if I am right, he does nothing lightly. Now then, I beg you to note that, in the circular letter to the prefects . . . you see, don't you see? . . . if he asks them to give aid and assistance to the Catholic clergy for a more effective Christianization of our popular masses, rural as well as urban—which can be understood only as a patient and peaceful work . . . uh . . . uh . . . you see . . . of a spiritual sanitation, in a way—nowhere do we see him prescribing the use of public force for brutal and coercive ends. . . ."

"Excuse me, gentlemen," said Madame Origène sweetly.

Like a basalt divinity of imposing form, disguised as a peasant to test the illustrious company, the Mayor's wife, whose name was Eudovia, stood powerfully on the threshold of the little cottage that served as the kitchen.

"Mac, dear," she said in a drawling voice that contrasted with the majesty of her bearing, "the coffee is ready, yes. Would you like it now?"

"Naturally," replied the Mayor impatiently. "You don't need, madame, to interrupt our conversation for such a trifle."

Being a sober man who knew how to control himself

in public and in private, he would never have shown such a reaction under different circumstances. Above all, he prided himself on the most distinguished propriety. But that day he felt a delicious elasticity in his tongue; it yielded joyfully to the ramblings of a meditative, studied elocution stuffed with incidental clauses; the sentences meekly followed the tortuous stream of his thought, slipping at the meanders, breaking at the falls, then converging again into a safe course. And now, right in the middle of a scientific exposition, scientifically developed . . . uh . . . uh . . . don't you see? . . .

"Oh-oooh!" said Madame Origène, without losing any of her placidity. "Oh-oooh! Don't tell me. Really, I don't know what's the matter with him today. You'd think it was the first time Mac had company! Could it be, poor devil, that Father Le Bellec's strong words are bothering him? Because, my friends, I can't believe that a single bottle of rum for three strong men . . . oh-oooh! . . . and I know how he can drink!"

"Well, all right! all right, madame!" broke in the Mayor, extremely angry. "While you're at it, you may as well say, once for all, that I'm a drunkard, a . . . a . . . you see . . . a tafia drinker, what, a rascal! . . . uh . . . uh . . . Disgrace me in front of these gentlemen! Take me apart from head to foot!"

Smiling, Madame Origène walked up to the table, took the bottle, and raising it to the level of her eyes, looked through it.

"That's just what I thought!" she said, continuing her teasing. "But why didn't you tell me it was empty, my little cat, instead of getting so excited? I'd have replaced it already, because, thank goodness, I'm not low on rum in the shop."

Macdonald Origène raised his eyes to heaven to express futility. Without paying any attention to it, his irreverent spouse called inside: "Alcius!"

Receiving no answer, she raised her voice a little: "Where did he go, the little nigger?"

"Here I am, yes, Godmother!" replied a handsome sixteen-year-old boy as he came from the kitchen. He was apparently well fed but poorly dressed in a pair of worn shorts and a little shirt too short for him that showed his navel sticking out like a baby penis on a slightly rounded belly with the skin taut like the cover of a drum.

"Where were you, good-for-nothing, that you couldn't answer me?" she asked. "Were you licking the plates?"

"Oh, Godmother!" protested the boy, looking sad. "Don't say that, no! That's something a kid would do, and it's more than three years now since my first communion."

She looked him up and down by way of reply.

"I don't mean to be disrespectful to the company, no, but I ask the Virgin Altagracia to strike me blind in both eyes if I'm lying, Godmother," swore poor Alcius in desperation.

"Go get the coffee for these gentlemen," she said coldly.

Then mockingly, as she winked at Macdonald Origène: "Alcius, put a bottle of rum on the tray."

She flashed her teeth in a generous smile and their dazzling fresh whiteness, like a pearl necklace, lit up the ebony of her face, and she withdrew with calm, heavy step as she had entered. So, as a courteous humanist, Septimus Morency felt like praising her as he did at every opportunity by bestowing on her the gracious epithet with which the Greeks honored Hera, the goddess with the large eyes: "Bovine Eudovia!"

He checked himself, however, considering the tenseness of the moment.

II

"Yes, that's how they all are nowadays!" said Bellami in order to console the Mayor, whose contorted face showed the suffering of the loser. "They don't have any respect for their husbands any more. But still, yours, my dear Mac, is only teasing you. That's not too serious. Besides, everyone knows she admires you. You should hear my little woman . . . The way she insults me for the slightest criticism of her behavior! She even goes so far sometimes as to call me a *negro sucio!*" He sighed, shaking his head, and continued: "Dirty nigger! Can you understand that, my friends? I can beat her, chastise her, all in vain, it makes no difference at all. I'm really beginning to think she loves to be beaten and that it's exactly what she wants. Because, after all, not only did I save her life, but I also dress and feed her like a princess! And I'm not counting all the beer I have to buy her. . . ."

While Lieutenant Charles-Oscar Bellami enumerated his marital troubles, Macdonald Origène was coldly considering his inexpressive head. Once again it irresistibly evoked the image of a well-scrubbed, brushed poodle, with lackluster, submissive eyes.

If he hadn't gone and picked her up in a brothel in Port-au-Prince! thought the Mayor uncharitably. So he has to punish her every time she feels the masochistic need for it. Otherwise she'll leave him one of these days for another male, one more given to flagellation, who will transport her to seventh heaven by treating her like the lowest of the low. To tell the truth, it would be good riddance for Charles-Oscar. But most likely he would take it as a disgrace, a misfortune, and sink into despair: the man only goes for mulatto females with a long mane . . . uh . . . uh . . . the Dominicans, especially . . . you have to pay the price!

Thus reasoned the Mayor of Boischandelle; but he declared, philosophically: "The thing is not as new as you think, dear friend. If I'm not mistaken, it was that genius, Napoleon, himself . . . I believe . . . who said at St. Helena, on his deathbed . . . uh . . . uh . . . you see . . . that a hero is never a great man to his valet."

Knowing that the Lieutenant would not catch the allusion to the infidelities of his perverse partner, of which, despite his well-known jealousy, he was the only one to be unaware, the Mayor, with a hypocritically saddened look, went on: "What would he have said of women, that brilliant captain, the most famous of all time . . . you see, don't you see? . . . if he had known how the seductive Josephine, despite her Creole non-chalance . . . uh . . . uh . . . had cuckolded him?"

A superior spirit, sovereignly indifferent to the base contingencies of married life ("*Aquila non capit muscas,*" he liked to say to justify his celibacy and the fact, odd for a single man, that he had no mistresses and that he only hired for the care of his house maids of all work of canonical age), Septimus Morency had given only distracted and amused attention to the conversation: *de minimis non curat praetor!*

"After all, Mayor Origène, to get back to the subject— and far be it from me to scrutinize too closely the whole bulk of your arguments, for your thinking is absolutely *ex professo*—I'll agree *in limine litis* that your analytical exegesis seems closely to embrace the august and monumental lines of the presidential thought with the clinging fidelity of the climbing ivy. But please enlighten me: on what, good God, do you establish the edificial foundation of your unpropitious verdict, when, *coram populo,* you accuse the Reverend Father Le Bellec of Catilinism?"

"It's very simple," said the Mayor, pouring coffee into the cups while Alcius waited patiently with arms folded, though he felt sad at the thought of the Pentecostalist hymns he was missing because of the extended meal. On Sunday afternoons, when he had time off, he always got dressed up and went to the Protestant church, which was also attended by the most virtuous among the young beauties of the region, Hortense Joseph, with whom he had formed a chaste, affectionate friendship.

"It's very simple," repeated Macdonald Origène. "You are not unaware, Justice Sèpe. . . . Will you have rum with it?"

"Just a teardrop . . . or rather, as specified by the medaled label of the cylindrical amphora: a drop of gold, dear friend, just a drop!"

"And you, Charles-Oscar?"

"I'll have the same as Justice Sèpe . . . 'to avoid any conflict!' " replied the officer with a mischievous, good-natured smile, alluding to a comic adventure that had happened to the Justice of the Peace in the past and that the latter willingly liked to recount as dazzling testimony of his skill at getting out of a tight spot.

(Septimus was the first to be amused by it, savoring the absurdity of the situation: "It was in the humiliating decades of the national martyrology when the soldiery Yankee, arrogant plenipotentiary of the materialistic barbariousness of utilitarian Anglo-Saxonism was defiling with rough boots and in full security the aristocratically spiritualistic and Mediterranean soil of our terrestrial patrimony," he said eloquently and by way of prelude. But then his face took on a gay look and he expressed himself less nobly, almost in the language of the common people: "One evening, after having chivalrously accomplished the ritual befitting prenuptial love —for I was then at the point of marriage—I was peacefully going back to my familial home, when an individual spontaneously emerged from the sinister shadow of a dark porch. From his khaki vestments as well as his zigzaggy walk, I spotted as the crow flies that it was an intemperant Marine totally under the delirious influence of distilled cane juice. In witness whereof dame Prudence, the tutelary companion of the meditative sage, urgently counseled me to move away from the uncertain route of this New Yorker on a spree; just then, the zebra, quicker than lightning, presented to me the *corpus delicti*—a fragrant and persuasive 'Five Star.'

" 'Say, boy, have a l'il drink wi' me.'

" 'Listen!' was my fast retort, parrying his presumptuous imperialism with a most categoric *noli me tangere.* 'Listen, Mister American, no naughty familiarity!'

" 'Well, well, if you no wanna drink wi' me, boy, me, I kill you.'

"And he started to reach for his pistol.

" 'In that case,' I said, quickly grabbing hold of the flask, 'in that case, Mister American, to avoid any conflict . . .' "

And the Justice of the Peace burst out in a hearty self-satisfied laugh, which invariably won over his audience.)

"Justice Sèpe, you are not unaware," resumed the Mayor, "that our beloved Chief, not at all satisfied with the evangelizing action of the French clergy, which he judges as inefficient . . . and even inadequate . . . for, in short, over the eighty years or more that we have had the concordat . . . isn't it so? . . . uh . . . uh . . . You are not unaware, I say, that the President of the Republic decided, in all wisdom, to introduce some priests from North America . . . oblates, as they are called . . . in the diocese of the South. They are all of Canadian origin and French-speaking. The Chief saw them there and found that they were accomplishing magnificent work in the United States . . . even edifying, one might say . . . full of sacrifice! So that our Breton priests . . . uh . . . uh . . . take a dim view of the presidential proceedings. For so long they've considered the country their private game preserve which they make no bones about calling 'Black Brittany' . . . you realize. . . . Hence, they are prepared to go to any length to defend their *de facto* monopoly, which they hold as a sacred right . . . uh . . . uh . . . And there's the hidden motive of the whole thing, Sèpe, dear friend, the very heart of the matter."

"As you have so graciously made the impartial though hypothetical remark, I am not unaware, Mayor Origène. And in fact, several moons ago already, a confidential hierarch breathed the criterionistic vibration of it into the auditory auricle of my jurisdictional, if not political, hearing. However, I do not see the umbilical cord that would congenitally unite the work of spiritual sanitation (to repeat your luminously specific definition) with the jealous irritation of the tonsured workers of the Breton beehive, who, if I understand you correctly, are seething with criminal plots leading conclusively to subterranean Catilinism. Now, this virulent and cardinal implication confuses both my analytical and judicious faculties."

"Septimus, dear friend," said the Mayor, "it seems to me that your natural good faith blinds you, that it prevents you from tracking down the tortuous ways of these priests . . . uh . . . uh . . . you see . . . and from unmasking their subtle Machiavellism. For, after all, I'd like to believe that you are not unaware of the fact that, under the abusive banner of this anti-superstition campaign, they have formed bands of fanatics . . . the Soldiers of St. Michael . . . don't you see? . . . and that, in certain places, these troublemongers have committed acts of violence against an interesting part of the population and harassed not only the vodou believers . . . uh . . . uh . . . but also, very often, the Protestants."

"Yes, indeed!" said Lieutenant Bellami with authority.

"Granted, dear friends, gr-anted!" said the Justice of the Peace. "I will not contest the joint veracity of your testimonial utterances. And I would even bring to the righteous floor of our courteous controversy the thought that the positivist tangibility of the facts deposed, in their undeniable congruence, does not lend itself to the methodic doubt of St. Thomas. However . . . for there is a 'but'—a *sed,* as the eminent professor of the Chair of Ciceronian Latinism might say . . . I do not yet spot the umbilical link—even genetic, one should specify with the mathematician pertinence of the modern scientist—which would biologically unite these absolutely statistical data with the anaerobic plot of a conspirational criminology."

Pretending deep discouragement, Macdonald Origène vigorously shook his head. Then he considered his interlocutor and a pitying smile brushed his fleshy complacent lips. "You don't see the unbilical cord, you say, Justice Sèpe . . . uh . . . uh . . . you don't see it! Well, I'm going to show it to you. It is quite simply the logical union, the fallacious connection existing between the circular letter to the prefects of the Republic on the one hand . . . uh . . . uh . . . you see . . . and, on the other, the punitive expeditions organized by the Breton fathers in their so-called anti-superstition campaign, and not anti-vodou . . . which, let it be said in passing, explains a number of things. . . ."

"Q.E.D.," cried Septimus Morency, treacherously interrupting the Mayor. "Dear friend, that's precisely what, by A plus B, you have to show us."

"I'll do it directly," replied Macdonald Origène with scornful assurance.

Thereupon, he made a long exposé from which it emerged that in claiming presidential authorization to commit acts of violence against the Protestant and vodou worshippers, the only aim of the Breton priests was to rouse the anger of the people against the Chief of State, with the hope that after the fall of the government it would be neither seen nor heard of and that consequently they would wash their hands of all the evils resulting from their subversive action, for the new "mentor" of the nation, forewarned of the danger inherent in the proposal . . . you see . . . would drop, once for all, the project concerning the oblates from New England.

"There is no doubt, no, my friends, that there is a real plot in that affair!" said Lieutenant Bellami, completely convinced.

"A con-spir-a-cy!" specified the Mayor energetically.

"There is no doubt, no!" repeated the officer, more and more filled with patriotic indignation.

"A real conspiracy, I tell you, Bellami! Besides, you are not unaware . . . uh . . . uh . . . that in high places they attribute to them a secret affiliation with the unnatural party of Marshall Pétain."

"As for that, Mayor Origène, you can say that again!"

"And I give as material proof of their anti-democratic hostility, the provocative action, harmful even, I must add, of His Excellency the Papal Nuncio . . . that Italian fascist . . . don't you see? . . . who went purposely to the neighboring republic, our historic adversary, if not hereditary enemy . . . you realize . . . to declare to the international journalists, without rhyme or reason . . . uh . . . uh . . . that the Haitian people are nothing but a savage pack of vodou-worshipping idolaters!"

"*Ad usum Delphini!*" feebly protested the Justice of the Peace, whose eloquence was visibly running out. "*Ad usum Delphini!* And I might even postulate: *jus et norma loquandi!* For it is not this acephalous terminology, partially guillotined of all nobiliary bearing, that the eminent Ambassador of His Holiness, recently misled into the slanderous duplicity of Hispanic totalitarianism, now struck with territorial excommunication by the touchy patriotism of our rightfully offended Presidency . . ."

"If they aren't his exact words, Justice Sèpe," said the

Mayor, inexorable and pedestrian, "at least, that's the true sense of his shameless declaration to the denigrating press of the bordering country and the other despisers of the sons of Ham. And all that . . . you see, don't you see? . . . the whole perverse maneuver . . . uh . . . uh . . . you realize . . . all that, treacherously taking advantage of the circular to the prefects!"

"Very strong, dear friend, very strong!" Septimus Morency ventured timidly as Madame Origène appeared at one of the windows of the house, completely filling the opening with her Junoesque bulk.

"Pardon, gentlemen!" she said with honeyed voice.

His wife's mocking smile augured more teasing; the Mayor frowned. "Now what, madame? We don't need coffee or rum."

Speaking low and as though she were conveying a confidential message, she announced: "Father Le Bellec is in the living room, yes."

"Father Le Bellec!" exclaimed the Mayor, astounded.

"He himself, in person!" confirmed Madame Origène, still ironically.

And she added with a sigh: "He says he has to talk to you about a serious matter!"

Macdonald Origène manfully straightened his trousers, poured himself a full glass of Barbancourt and drank it down, then finally got up.

"I'm going," he said laconically.

It did not take him long to come back. But the shiny black of his face, with angles like coal, had turned the cold gray of a corpse; his eyes fairly popped out of their sockets. He fell into a chair, quickly loosened his tie, opened his shirt collar, and let out his belt, blowing like a seal.

All at once, Madame Origène lost her serenity. She

rushed as fast as her buxom body permitted, armed with the cover of a shoebox, and with rapid movements of which one would have thought her incapable, she fanned all around the Mayor's head as he was making efforts to talk and could not articulate a single word—so true is it, as the proverb tells us, that when a word is too strong our jaw aches.

"Give him a comforting cordial instead, dear friend, for according to the infallible therapy of the Romans, *bonum vinum laetificat cor hominis*," solemnly said Septimus Morency, not forgetting his Latin.

"Yes, Madame Origène, some rum with a grain of salt to dissolve the bad blood," added Bellami, worried.

But the Mayor was already regaining his composure.

"Uh . . . uh," he said very low, his tongue still thick. "Propose that to me . . . do you realize . . . and to set a good example, he had the nerve to tell me!"

"What's that, old friend?" asked the Justice of the Peace, with compassion.

"Propose to me that I 'reject' vodou, to me, Macdonald Origène . . . as though I were . . . uh . . . uh . . . the last of the idolaters of the commune . . . you see . . . of Boischandelle!"

Then, suddenly getting his strength back: "I showed him the door!"

III

The following Saturday, as usual, Madame Origène, returning from market, had taken off her wide straw hat in front of the oval mirror in the dining room. Her eyes sparkling with coquetry, her face both attentive and placid, she was tying a scarlet polka-dot kerchief on her head while her austere spouse, comfortably stretched out in a rocking chair near the front door, "scrutinized" with delight the newspapers from Port-au-Prince which Rénélus Altidor, the punctual driver of the Boar of the Mountain, had just delivered to him.

As in everything he did, the Mayor of Boischandelle proceeded slowly, methodically, and with a peculiar sense of hierarchy in which the instinct of symmetry figured strongly and tyrannically: first the political life of the country and the anti-superstition campaign; then the sciences, literature, and the arts, the social events; and finally, the war—that great collective folly which, fortunately . . . uh . . . uh . . . you realize . . . raged in faraway places.

"Do you know, Mac, that I saw Estinval this morning?" said Madame Origène suddenly, in her most innocent way. "He was leaving the parsonage."

"Estinval!" said the Mayor, with a start. And he took off his pince-nez. "But, but, but . . . if I'm not mistaken you mean that phony of a father of yours . . . Estinval Civilhomme, called Dr. Lhomme . . . the vodou priest of Fonds-Rouge . . . uh . . . uh . . . don't you?"

"One can't hide a thing from you, my dear," she replied, with a sweetly ironic smile. "But there is one thing, surely, that you can't possibly guess. Estinval is going to 'reject'!"

"Estinval, really, Madame Origène?"

"Himself, in person, Mayor Origène, and no later than two weeks from Sunday, after the six o'clock Mass." She added with an air of false consternation: "With all the *pitites-caille!*"

"You mean . . . uh . . . uh . . . don't you, do you . . . with his acolytes and clientele?"

"Beg your pardon, Mayor Origène?"

"He's going to 'reject' with the members of his confraternity and with his patients?"

"Exactly, Mayor!"

"We'll have seen everything in this poor country!" sighed the Mayor, who felt he must be dreaming. And he certainly had reason to be astonished. As a *houngan,* Estinval Civilhomme earned a good living treating illnesses supposed to be supernatural. Could one logically conceive that he would voluntarily give up such a lucrative profession? And . . . can you imagine . . . just for love of an insignificant little priest . . . uh . . . uh . . . can you imagine that? "And he didn't mention it to me, the rascal . . . didn't breathe a word! A man, you see . . . or rather, to better express my thought . . . a fraud, a charlatan . . . and he tells anyone who'll listen . . . uh . . . uh . . . that he was trained by the Masters of the Water, that mythical product of the popular imagination!"

It was true, however, that when he was about twelve years old, Estinval had mysteriously disappeared from the region of Boischandelle. His mother had sent him to fill the calabashes at the spring of Fonds-Rouge and he had not come back until seven years later, endowed with a necklace of real pearls. At first he did not want to say anything about where he had been and what he had been doing all that time. But soon he began to effect astonishing recoveries, curing mental ills, yaws, and tuberculosis, and the rumor spread quickly, although no one knew how it started, that during his long absence Estinval had lived "beneath the waters" in the magic world of the spirits with the blue eyes who haunt the swamps, pools, and rivers, and that it was one of them who had taught him the healing properties of plants and had transmitted to him the power of sending the dead back to the cemetery and appeasing the African gods.

"A charlatan!" repeated the Mayor of Boischandelle, who, officially at least, did not admit the existence of the marvelous in modern times, though it be Christian. "An accomplished fraud . . . uh . . . uh . . . you see? . . . And now he claims, doesn't he . . . that he is going to 'reject' his whole kit and caboodle of sorcery. I am wondering what Machiavellian motive is behind his maneuver. Could he be in cahoots with the Breton clergy to sow the seeds of discord . . . and overthrow the government . . . uh . . . uh . . . could he? They have worked hand in glove so long on the financial level . . . tacitly, it's true . . . but for their greater profit. . . . I'm wondering what interest the aquatic spirits could possibly have in this scheme. Estinval . . .

27

as far as I know, you see . . . has never worshipped them at all . . . uh . . . uh . . . not even the sacrifice of an ordinary chicken. . . . But, since he did not erect an altar to them, he won't need to renounce them . . . and their secret business can undoubtedly continue . . . as though nothing had happened. . . . That's the whole crux of the matter!"

Macdonald Origène could boast all he wanted that he was a Cartesian, he kept on being impressed by the surprising cures the *houngan* effected. When he was a child, his nurse had many times told him that at the time of the massacre of the colonists, God, who always takes care of his own, had permitted the "good whites" to hide in caves with their slaves, and that when these chosen people died, they became masters of all the bodies of water in Haiti. He no longer believed in this legend, but it lay buried in his subconscious, so that he often seemed to hear, rising out of the past, the singing muted voice of the nurse and he always had to struggle to withstand its power and not to revert, as he so greatly feared, to the superstition of his childhood.

On the other hand, if he were to believe his father-in-law's followers, it was absolutely certain that a white woman appeared to Estinval in the form of a ravishing bather. Since she was blond and radiant like a Holy Virgin on an almanac, and was combing her long hair with a golden comb, Estinval knew instantly that he was in the presence of a supernatural being. He was so awestricken he dropped his calabashes on the pebbles in the path, where they broke. At first he was dismayed because the disaster clearly merited some punishment and his father's hand was quite harsh; then tears came to his eyes and he began to sob.

When she saw this, the bather asked him: "Are you afraid you'll be whipped?"

He nodded yes and showed his despair more than ever, thinking that the white lady, moved by pity, would put back together by some magic the calabashes which, in his disarray, he had foolishly broken.

"Since that's the way it is," she said, "come with me. In my country we never beat children."

She took him by the hand and led him to the grotto close by the spring, and from there they went down beneath the waters toward the dazzling city of the spirits with the blue eyes.

This tale of the marvelous has never been doubted by good people, but the skeptics, the jealous, and the gossips, although they did not discredit the vision or the breaking of the calabashes, suggested a more materialistic version, according to which Estinval simply started running when he saw the Mistress of the Water. Then, to get out of the spanking he deserved, he went to Port-au-Prince, where he lived miserably as a vagabond begging his food until the day the police picked him up for theft and locked him up in the reformatory. After two or three years as an inmate, he escaped from the institution with the son of a well-known *houngan* from Croix-des-Missions. And eventually, finding exceptional talents in him, this vodou priest initiated and trained him in the priesthood along with his own son.

As for the famous necklace which he wore when he officiated in his *houmfor* or treated the sick, and which he said the Spirits of the Water had given him, either the pearls were false or he had acquired them in an illicit way, for just before Estinval's return to Fonds-Rouge, a jewelry store in Port-au-Prince had been burglarized. . . . Of course, he was not accused of having committed the theft himself, but he might well have bought the jewel for a low price from the thief himself or from a receiver, and his enemies, even the most rabid, favored this hypothesis.

"A charlatan, I tell you, Madame Origène!" continued the Mayor, and he raised his voice energetically so he would not hear the insidious voice of the nurse. "An impostor . . . not to say a swindler . . . uh . . . uh . . . you realize!"

But whatever the truth of the matter, for Estinval's followers as for most of the inhabitants of the commune, it was this necklace that gave him second sight and dictated to him what medications to prescribe. And so, as the years went by, he became the most influential personage of the region. He was not feared however, but respected; not being a sorcerer, he did not practice evil. And willy-nilly, closing their eyes, the priests did not forbid him admittance to the church—although he was not admitted at holy communion—and he often went there to pray.

He owed this favor mostly to Madame Origène, his favorite daughter, who was brought up in the parsonage of Boischandelle, whence divine grace had led her when she was still very young. And this is another story, although it flows directly from the preceding one.

IV

Eudovia had once confided to Macdonald Origène that as far back as she could remember they often told stories in the evening about the country of the Spirits of the Water, where, although you never see the sun, it is always day. Her father had lived there, they told her, in a large city built entirely of marble, with beautiful gardens and spacious avenues planted with fruit trees; and she never stopped dreaming about it.

And so, when she was old enough to carry a calabash full of water on her head, every morning she went to the spring at Fonds-Rouge with the naïve hope that she would meet a beautiful white lady there who would surely take her beneath the waters and after seven years give her a pearl necklace with which she could treat supernatural ills just like her father.

Instead of the blond lady bathing, it was an albino, a white Negro, who finally appeared to her. She found him so hideous that then and there she fled as fast as her legs would carry her, crying and screaming, but taking back the calabashes, which, despite her fright, she had not dropped on the pebbles in the path.

31

When Eudovia told her what had happened, she almost took Madame Civilhomme's breath away.

"How stupid you are!" she cried when she recovered from her astonishment. "You should have followed him, child; it was for your own good."

"Han-han?" said Eudovia, sarcastically. "Then why was he as ugly as a tawny owl?"

"Why, child?" answered Madame Civilhomme, hesitating. "How should I know that, myself? All I can tell you is that next time you see him at the spring . . ."

"Well, no, Mama!"

Eudovia shook her head, precociously showing the quiet will and strength which later on were to constitute the dominant traits of her character and which one felt were unyielding, inaccessible to either constraint or sweetness.

"Well, no. I don't want to go to a country where the people are as ugly as that. I don't want to. The Masters of the Water are so awfully white they look as though they have no skin!"

She suddenly recalled the grotesque person with his blinking eyes and no eyelashes, with his bloodless mouth, and she hid her face in her hands, crying: "Ugh, how repulsive!"

After that she refused to go fill the calabashes at the spring. She had been so upset that she showed indifference and even disdain toward everything that had any connection at all with the Spirits of the Water, including the magic necklace that gave Estinval so much prestige.

Some time later, as she was being taught that the illnesses from which her father's patients suffered were inflicted on them by the *mystères* as a punishment for their sins—mostly venial and sometimes even involuntary, such as a promise wrung from someone in a dream or the failure to fulfill a ritual duty because of poverty or some other obstacle—Eudovia revolted.

"So," she said bluntly, "so, as I see them, your *loas* are nothing but a bad lot—harmful beings and evildoers!"

The boldness of the remark shook the members of the family out of their wits and they foresaw the worst calamities from it. To teach her a lesson and to appease the wrath of the *mystères*, who are always ready to assert their power, her father beat her until he drew blood. She wept, to be sure, but silently, and she showed no repentance, thus sustaining the panic she had caused in the family. Then, in the vain hope of breaking down her resolve, they took her for the first time to visit the little huts where Estinval housed his patients; but, instead of impressing her, the sight of the sickly and the demented only strengthened in her mind the subversive idea that the *mystères* were evil-doing spirits, in a word, devils, *je-renonce.* And she made the awesome vow that whatever befell her, adversity or happiness, she would never serve them.

As a consequence, that same night, Our Lady of the Seven Sorrows appeared to her in a dream.

Since she resembled one of those religious images that filled her father's *houmfor* and were identified with the principal vodou divinities of the popular religion, Eudovia frowned and was ready to spit in her face. But, aware that the child mistook her for Mistress Erzilie, the goddess of love, and that her mistake was due to the error in which her parents had brought her up, the Virgin said to her with a smile: "You have been deceived, my little one. I am not a *mystère,* no. I am the Mother of Jesus Christ."

Then she took Estinval's daughter in her arms and comforted her.

Eudovia felt an indescribable sensation from this miraculous contact—something between fear and joy emanating from her body like an overflow, gradually changing into an infinite, almost superhuman sweetness, in its damp warmth.

"Tomorrow you will leave your father's house," said the Virgin finally, before laying the child back on her mat. "But you will not go, as he did, to the Masters of the Water. You will go directly to the parsonage at Boischandelle and tell the old priest that it was I, myself in person, who sent you to him so that he would take you in and bring you up in my Son's religion."

Shivering from the early-morning chill, Eudovia opened her eyes in a bad mood, annoyed to find herself in the cruel world of the *loas*. But she soon understood, feeling wet, that reality was in keeping with her dream, thus confirming that the visit of Our Lady of the Seven Sorrows had truly taken place. So great was her joy that she paid no attention to the fact, however disturbing, that her bed exuded the usual proof of her nocturnal lapses, an acid musky odor. Force of habit protected her innocent nose from a perception that, on the whole, could hardly delight it.

Though he had no knowledge of this equivocal detail, the good Father Saintyves, parish priest at the time, was not rash enough to believe that the dream had been sent by God and was a miracle. He was, to tell the truth, a robust peasant from Ille-et-Vilaine with very simple ideas, who had modestly taken the road to heaven with both feet squarely on the ground. But despite the fact that he was not a Doctor of Divinity, he was well aware of the great caution the Church observes toward facts of

34

this nature and the prudent doubt and systematic mistrust that it applies to verify them.

On the other hand, Eudovia Civilhomme, who was just turning eight, had not the vaguest notion about these edifying marvels. And all she asked was to be taken into the parsonage to get away from the awful hold of vodou—which permitted abstracting from the problem the thorny implications of a mystic nature and considering it from its immediate earthly and somewhat more human aspect.

Father Saintyves reduced it to this practical question: how to satisfy Eudovia's impassioned plea, which he wholeheartedly approved. Of course, he said to himself, it was not clear that Our Lady of the Seven Sorrows had sent the child to him; but was it not written that the ways of the Lord are mysterious, and could he refuse the succor of charity to whomsoever asked? The only delicate point was to obtain the consent of Eudovia's father, whom he held, rightly or wrongly, as an instrument of hell.

Having thoughtfully considered the pros and cons, Father Saintyves sent him his maid—the wily Velléda, who had the gift of gab and used the dialectic resources of Creole to perfection—for, worthy neighbor of the cunning Normans that he was, he thought that pious purposes must sometimes put up with a bit of guile—a way, after all, of turning his favorite weapon against the Evil One.

But it was just a matter of pushing against an open door. Velléda got Estinval's consent without a fight. Joining his hands devoutly and raising his eyes to heaven as his face expressed strong satisfaction, the *houngan* declared: "Since the Holy Virgin saw fit to guide

Eudovia to God's house, I can only rejoice. My daughter is in better hands than mine."

And, of course, one could hardly claim that Estinval was not being consistent, considering, as he often proclaimed, that he always "worked" with our Holy Mother the Church—and he could have added that he contributed to her prosperity to the extent that, in order to realize their full effect, his cures had to be topped off with a Mass of thanksgiving, thus assuring the parish of Boischandelle the best part of its income. But from that to rejecting! thought Macdonald Origène, inwardly sneering, . . . uh . . . uh . . . a big gap, isn't it?

As we know, he suspected some trickery behind it and dreaded the payoff, for, on the one hand, as Mayor, prudence and loyalty required his siding with the government, and on the other, they recommended that he not alienate himself from the protection of Estinval, whose influence on the inhabitants of the region assured his political fortune. And, as if the complexity of the facts was not enough to torment him, here, plain to see and for the first time since their marriage . . . you realize . . . Eudovia was not on his side!

"And so, Mac," she asked anxiously, "don't you think that's good news?"

"Uh . . . uh . . . what?" he asked, taken aback.

"What I've just told you about Estinval."

"That he is going to . . . going to . . . reject?" said the Mayor of Boischandelle, his voice choked with indignation.

"Yes, Mayor Origène. As for me, I'm so happy I don't know what to do. Because, after all, it's not for nothing that I've been praying to God since I was a child," she explained with a youthful smile.

And she said it sincerely, without the least trace of irony, although she knew that Estinval's conversion, at least the way he was going about it, displeased the Mayor because it put him on the spot. But wasn't that a small price to pay for the redemption of a sinner? she thought. After all, giving him credit for a great deal of learning, she deeply admired her husband, and if she sometimes teased him, it was out of modesty and to hide the tenderness she felt for the spouse she loved both as a hero and as a child . . . for, good heavens, aren't all men like children in the practical matters of life?

But since he'd had disappointments in his youth as everyone does, and they had left him with an instinctive distrust of the fair sex, Macdonald Origène was close to crying treason and proclaiming that his old friend Senator Aristhène was quite right in saying that the Haitian woman is her husband's Achilles' heel, when there was a knock at the door.

It was Estinval.

V

"Greetings, son," said the old man simply as he took off his hat.

"Good morning, Dr. Lhomme," replied Macdonald Origène coldly, without bothering to get up. "How are you?"

"Not too bad, son. And you?"

"Oh so-so, thank goodness."

"I'm just dropping in to see you for a moment. Some important business brought me to town this morning. . . . Did Eudovia tell you?"

Macdonald Origène sat up, very much the Mayor of Boischandelle, and assumed an offended air. "It's . . . isn't . . . isn't it . . . ?"

His son-in-law seemed so enraged that Estinval was wide-eyed with astonishment.

"So it's true . . . uh . . . uh . . . that you are going to *reject?*"

"Positively," replied the old man, casually seating himself in a mahogany rocker.

Then, distractedly stroking his goatee, whose cottony whiteness—in contrast to his small mobile eyes, shrewd and illusionless—gave his features a reassuring look, marked by sweetness and goodheartedness: "Every day is a day, son, but Monday is not Tuesday. And, as you know, I've always stood for progress."

"You are not unaware," said Macdonald Origène harshly, "that the government of His Excellency the President of the Republic . . . you see . . . don't you see . . . highly motivated by its patriotic duty toward the popular masses of the country . . ."

"I know," said Estinval, to cut short any scientific exposé, for Eudovia had already briefed him. "I haven't come as a spokesman for Father Le Bellec. And, son, I'm not the one to advise you to betray your Chief. Never! Such as I am, I am all for one's honor, and I think that one ought always behave honorably if he deserves to be called a man. Only, if you'll permit me a little remark, I'll tell you that governments come and go, while our Holy Mother the Catholic Church, apostolic and Roman, is always present among us, firmly planted on its two legs and with far-reaching arms."

"What's that, Dr. Lhomme!" exclaimed Macdonald Origène, relieved (because, after all . . . he did . . . didn't he . . . the old macaque did understand the delicacy of his position . . . uh . . . uh . . . you see!) and amused at the thought that his father-in-law, though he had not read Claudel, since he was virtually illiterate, easily expressed himself in the sanctimonious catechism-class style which this great Christian voice affected out of defiance—or was it humility?—when he switched to a rustic simplicity. "What's that, Dr. Lhomme, you talking to me like this . . . you, yourself . . . a *houngan* . . . a . . . a *boccor* . . . a . . . a sorcerer!"

Although he always tried to check his impatience,

Estinval shook his head and showed his discouragement. "First, son, let me tell you once for all: I am not a *houngan,* much less a *boccor.* All my life I've fought superstition."

"No!" said the Mayor. "You don't say!"

"I've always been a faithful servant of God's," specified Estinval.

Macdonald Origène felt like bursting out laughing; he let himself go. Now that was rash, for he had worked ever harder since his adolescence to eliminate from his behavior manifestations of this kind, which he judged incompatible with his idea of respectability. The result was a series of pitiful contortions that drew from his chest a painful cascade of raucous, cavernous sounds devoid of persuasive force, because the muscles which were to give expression to his amusement, from lack of exercise, could not coordinate to produce one of those outbursts of hilarity whose frankness and vigor would disarm the most obdurate adversary. So his facial muscles puckered up, translating their failure into a fixed and painful grin.

With a mocking air, Estinval had quietly waited for the end of this grotesque agitation. It avenged him so well for the feeling that had caused it that he could not be offended by it. In fact, he was close to feeling pity for his son-in-law.

"Ah, Dr. Lhomme!" sighed the Mayor of Boischandelle, completely unaware that he had been ridiculous, and regaining his good humor. "How amusing you are!" He dried his eyes complacently and confessed: "You almost made me choke."

"Yes, indeed," admitted Estinval. "But you'll agree there was no reason for it."

Macdonald Origène was starting to get excited again.

"No reason!" he said, his nostrils flaring. "You really think there was no reason?"

"Of course," answered Estinval.

"Then . . . you see . . . don't you see . . . I'm giving my tongue to the cat. For, in a word, on the one hand you say you are an enemy of superstition . . . a faithful servant of God . . . and on the other, you own a *houmfor* . . . a vodou temple . . . uh . . . uh . . . you openly make sacrifices to the *loas*. . . . Under the circumstances, therefore, I don't see how you are any different from a *houngan* . . . from an exploiter of the credulousness of the country's popular masses . . . don't you see?"

The old man tossed his head and ostensibly crossed his arms, as though he were having trouble containing himself. "I can easily see that you don't know what a *houngan* is. I'll have to explain it to you!"

"Go ahead, Dr. Lhomme, go ahead!" said the Mayor, polite and witty. "Don't worry about that at all. I'm all ears, you see . . . a rubberneck. . . . Out with your little speech . . . your claptrap, to be exact . . . uh . . . uh . . . isn't it . . . open up your bag of goods!"

"Thanks," said Estinval amiably, for although he did not catch the allusion, he got the derogatory tone and was playing innocent. "You know, son, that a *loa* cannot 'work' if he does not have a *horse* at his disposal. Well, that's a *houngan's* principal role—he is the *horse* of a *mystère* who himself, in this case, is called the 'master of the house.' . . . Now, then, suppose you want some good luck. What do you do? You go to consult a *houngan*. And what's the first thing he does? He takes you inside his *houmfor,* invokes the master of the house, who *mounts* him immediately and speaks through his mouth. The *mystère* then talks with you, states his conditions, and if you accept them, gives you what you asked for. As far as I, Estinval Civilhomme, am concerned, things never happen like that, because the house has no other master than myself. . . . First, I must tell you, what I learned beneath the waters goes far beyond the science the *houngans* claim. So I can assure you I am stronger than any of them . . . and even the whole lot together."

"I know all that, Dr. Lhomme . . . all that and even more. . . . I'm not a baby born yesterday morning . . . am I, now, am I? But, except for a difference in the amount of power, I still don't see . . . you understand . . . what could possibly distinguish you from the *houngans* . . . uh . . . uh . . . from the sorcerers. . . . Like them, you make sacrifices to the *loas*."

"But I haven't finished explaining it to you, son," said Estinval, patiently. "Just listen a while, and you'll finally understand."

"I'd be delighted, Dr. Lhomme. As I've just told you . . . uh . . . uh . . . haven't I . . . I'm all ears. . . . If I interrupt you sometimes . . . and I apologize for it . . . it's simply . . . don't you see . . . so you can clarify certain points of your interesting exposé which escape my rationalistic comprehension."

"Where do supernatural ills come from?" asked the old man. "Who else but the *mystères* can inflict them on living beings? How can you treat these ills unless you deal with those who have inflicted them? Because, as the proverb says, 'He who chained Bouqui is the one who'll set him free.' Let's suppose a sick man comes to consult me and I see that a dead man's spirit has been cast upon him to torment him. What must I do in such a situation? I must call Baron Samedi, who is the master of cemeteries, and ask him to take his thing and put it back where it belongs."

"And how do you call forth this sinister character . . . uh . . . uh . . . since you tell me the *loas* never *mount* you?"

"I have several *horses* at his disposal, poor souls who are completely under the domination of the *loas* and have come to me for protection."

"I see, Dr. Lhomme, I see!" said the Mayor ironically. "You may continue your scholarly dissertation."

"If it's a *service* that Baron Samedi requires as payment," said Estinval, "I perform it. Period, that's all. After that, I've nothing more to do with him, because I do not serve the *loas*. I only bargain with them for the release of the poor unfortunates they persecute. But as far as *houngans* are concerned, their luck, their money—in a word, all they possess—they get all these, every last one of them, from the master of their house. As I've told you, I don't have any. My knowledge, my possessions, my popularity, it's the Masters of the Water who have given me all of them—of course, with the good Lord's permission. . . . Do you understand the difference now, son?"

"To tell you the truth, Dr. Lhomme, fundamentally . . . basically, to express myself more precisely . . . you understand . . . uh . . . uh . . . I don't see any difference at all, since, in order to treat your patients, you have to make contact with the *loas,* those grotesque divinities of the African pantheon."

"Only for the supernatural ills, son! As for the others, I don't need to deal with any of these *je-renonce,* since they are not inflicted by them but are sent by God. And, as you know, I am a diviner. When a sick person comes

43

to see me, I can tell at first glance what the trouble is and what has to be done to cure him—with the help of the Lord, naturally. A *houngan* does not have this power. The master of the house has to find out what the illness is and show him how to treat it. Now, son, tell me frankly, isn't it clear to you that we are not the same, he and I?"

"On that level, Dr. Lhomme, I won't say no . . . you see . . . uh . . . uh . . . but, on the other . . . with respect to ills you call supernatural . . . you have business relations, in a way, with the *loas* . . . off and on, of course, sporadic . . . you make sacrifices to them . . . and consequently, I don't at all grasp how you can say you're an enemy of superstition. . . . But that concerns only your conscience . . . uh . . . uh . . . and its elasticity seems to me to be foolproof . . . and I'll not quibble with you over this delicate point . . . thorny, even, one might say . . . uh . . . uh . . . mightn't one? . . . What I'd like to know is what you're going to do once you've *rejected*. . . . Will you retire . . . which, just between us, seems a logical necessity, if not an ineluctable corollary . . . or will you keep on treating the sick as you have been doing?"

"Most certainly!" replied Estinval, without the least hesitation.

"That's just what I thought!" cried out the Mayor of Boischandelle, feeling like a prosecutor who has just forced a confession from the accused. "But then . . . you see . . . uh . . . uh . . . don't you . . . what's the point of your *rejecting?*"

Estinval seemed surprised at the question.

"What's the point? Why, to be a good example," he said, with conviction, "to help the Church conquer

44

superstition. For there is one thing you are not consider-ing. If all the people here *reject* the *mystères*—and I certainly hope they will—there would be no one left in the commune to serve them, to give them food and drink, and they would have no choice but to pack up and go elsewhere. Then too, by God's grace, I'd have only natural ills to contend with."

Then, smiling, with mischief in his eyes: "And by the same token, you would be satisfied. Right, son?"

The old macaque! The old macaque! thought Mac-donald Origène with delight, close to admiring him; but he was not yet willing to admit defeat.

"Good. Now tell me, Dr. Lhomme," he asked cau-tiously, "suppose there are some recalcitrant ones . . . you realize . . . people who refuse to follow your edi-fying example."

"I'll know how to put them on the right track. Be-cause there is something you don't seem to be aware of, and that's the fact that no one serves the *loas* gladly. They are too demanding. And aside from that, though you may do your duty by them, they never give you something for nothing when you ask for a little help in time of need. Hence people put up with them as a fatality, a heavy heritage bequeathed by the ancestors in Guinea. Most of the people here would be only too happy to get rid of them. In the past, when Catholic priests confined themselves to preaching the gospel, they did not know what could be done. Now things have changed, by God's grace. Our Holy Mother the Church has become vigorously active. Everyone is going to *reject*, I tell you."

"Everyone?" asked the Mayor, still doubtful.

"Except the jealous and ambitious ones, naturally.

Those who are up to their ears in black magic. And, as far as I know, there are only two of them hereabouts. Josaphat Joseph, the *boccor* from Bassin-Bleu . . ."

"Your competitor, isn't he?" asked Macdonald Origène, with a knowing smile. "Or, rather, to be exact, your adversary."

"And Boss Louis-Jean," said Estinval, firmly and without moving a muscle, as though he were throwing a trump card on the table. "Boss Louis-Jean Février, your political enemy, the Minister of the Interior's protégé, who carries on all kinds of intrigues to replace you as head of the Town Council."

He got up to leave, but since his son-in-law seemed perplexed and found nothing to say by way of reply, he added quite seriously, as a man for whom the future holds no secrets: "Only, you know, son, Boss Louis-Jean Février is absolutely nothing on his own. He depends on Josaphat, and Josaphat is a slave to the *mystères*. So that, when everyone has *rejected* and the *loas* have rid the region of their evil presence, neither Josaphat nor Boss Louis-Jean will be worth more than the dust on the highway. Furthermore, if you'll permit me to give you a bit of advice, I'll tell you to steer clear of the whole business. Tomorrow the government will make up with the Church, for, basically, it's no more than a husband-and-wife quarrel. Just a question of jealousy! And so, you understand, my dear Mac, you must not be the embarrassing witness."

As he talked, he had been making his way to the door.

"Goodbye, son," he said finally. "It's high time for me to go back up to Fonds-Rouge."

Then, looking outside: "It's clouding over. The rains will come soon."

VI

If Estinval was able to *reject* freely, it was not at all easy for the peasants of Boischandelle, even for those living in his immediate neighborhood. They had to ask permission of the African gods who were supposed to protect them and they could not obtain it without making costly offerings and sacrifices. As a result, the poorest among them had no choice but to remain under the tyrannical domination of the *mystères* or to go into debt for the rest of their lives.

It was a clear profit for Estinval, since he was the greatest usurer in the area; but his clients were completely hoodwinked. He was even able to convince them that his fees as a *houngan*—which were high, of course—barely paid him for such exhausting work. And, in fact, since he had to proceed on an individual basis, the liberation rites took him a whole week, at the end of which so many animals were sacrificed, from fowls to cattle, that the commune of Boischandelle was almost half depleted.

Besides, one had to admit, everything was done correctly, and, in general, everything went off as expected.

The *angels* and *saints* of the Arada cult, although they reacted with strong indignation, consented without much ado to free Estinval's clients from their obligations. And if the *devils* of the Pétro cult required a great deal of coaxing, it was only to extort more, for all of them gave up their privileges once their demands were met. Except Marinette Braschèche, to be sure—the impenitent ogress, the leper with the dried-up arms—who had demanded the sacrifice of a "goat without horns"; but this was her way, as they say, and no one was shocked by it, except for the obstinacy she showed in this instance. The incident was all the more serious because of the fact that the *horse* chosen by Marinette was none other than Man Yaya, Estinval's own wife, whom she rode roughly, to boot.

That day, however, knowing that she had assumed rights over his wife, whose allegiance she had extorted in a dream, Estinval had reserved the best for the ogress and had even been so obliging as to grant her preeminence in the hierarchy of the cult. And he had largely contributed to the expenses of the ceremony out of his own pocket.

The day before, he had two black chickens killed and ritually cooked for Marinette, as well as a young she-goat of the same color that no he-goat had yet mounted. And although the service was intended mainly for all the Pétro *mystères*, he had lit the infernal fire near the tree sacred to the she-devil.

Possessing Estinval's farm hands—three mysterious dwarfs he had hired no one knew where or how, and who, according to his enemies, belonged to the maleficent "little folk" of the *bakas*—Ti-Jean Pétro, Escalier Boumba, and Bacoulou Barac were already gaily dancing in the fire to the accelerating rhythm of the drums, while the *hounsis* sang under the direction of Man Yaya, who acted as *reine-chanterelle:*

> Ti-Jean Pétro, devil oh!
> Escalier Boumba, devil oh!
> Bacoulou Barac, devil oh!
> You have given me magic power.
> The power is too strong for me!
> I tell you I'm giving it up. . . .

This song was repeated several times with no letup. Then the beat of the drums became stronger, more pressing, and Man Yaya with outstretched arms cried out dramatically: "Ti-Jean-an!"

As he danced in the fire, leading Escalier Boumba and Bacoulou Barac in a fantastic hallucinating round that raised whirling clouds of sparks (a frenzy of diabolic glowworms in the throes of midnight revelry, one might think), Ti-Jean replied in a raucous voice that seemed to come from far off:

> What shall we do?
> Oh! What shall we do about that?
> Cayman comes up from the water,
> He tells us that Fish is sick!
> What shall we do?
> Oh! What shall we do about that?

The choir immediately resumed: "Ti-Jean Pétro, devil oh . . ." And while one of the drummers kept up the impetuous rhythm of the round, his partner was playing against the beat, with less speed but greater force, inviting the dancers to do the "feint."

The three devils stepped backwards out of the fire,

then went in again slowly, advancing the foot with a floating gesture, hesitantly, feeling their way furtively, all the while feigning to ward off blows, as though fighting enemies invisible to those in attendance.

And the round started up again in the fire, more vigorously than before, the *mystères* singing in unison with the choir:

> Oh! the Saint-Djo!
> The day has come,
> And I can say nothing!
> Sickness comes first, alas!
> Health afterwards!
> The day has come, alas!
> And I can say nothing!

Bringing her hands up to her face, Man Yaya staggered. They rushed to hold her up, but a convulsive tremor shook her from head to foot. The skin on her arms dried up and numerous nodules appeared; her fingers tightened into claws and her features gradually became deformed, finally assuming the leonine facies of a leper.

"Marinette!" sighed the attendants, swept by a long tremor.

With head bowed down, the she-devil cast a wary glance at the spectators. No one made haste to grant her the usual attention. With the exception of Estinval, it seemed as though everyone was taking root in the ground and turning to stone.

"Ladies and gentlemen, the society, good evening," she said finally in a raucous and almost plaintive voice.

"Good evening, yes, Mam'zelle Marinette!" they answered, forcing themselves to smile as best they could.

"So, my friends, that's the way it is now!" she said in a

very low voice, cunning and seemingly intimidated in her turn. "This is how I'm received in my *horse*'s house!"

"What are you grumbling about?" brusquely asked Estinval, who, with hands on his hips and a haughty air, had been observing her until that moment. "Aren't you our guest?"

"That's what I would have thought. But I am very thirsty, my friends, and no one is offering me so much as a little bottle of gas. And you know very well how fond I am of that beverage."

She smiled hideously, her lips parting with difficulty over her loose teeth. Estinval shrugged.

"You can never wait. You were brought up so badly, always asking for something!"

With nervous step he went to get a liter of kerosene in the *houmfor*. Then taking it to Marinette, he added dryly: "You see, we still have good manners in this house."

Avidly and without the least thanks, she took hold of the bottle, swallowed the contents in one gulp, and threw it on the fire, where the frenzied round of the dwarf demons was continuing, gayer than ever:

> The-house-cracks oh,
> Similor!
> It's me they call the-house-cracks oh,
> Similor!
> Oua, oua, yahou!
> The-house-cracks oh,
> Similor!
> It's me they call the-house-cracks oh,
> Similor!
> Oua, oua, yahou . . .

Suddenly, Marinette pivoted on herself as though she were drunk, howling as she turned. The drums vigorously started up again, triumphally sustained by the choir:

> Marinette Braschèche,
> Similor!
> Ti-Jean Pétro,
> Similor!
> Escalier Boumba,
> Similor!
> Bacoulou Barac,
> Similor!

Marinette rushed headlong into the fire, seized the red-hot iron bar that had been heating since the day before, kissed it devoutly and held it out to her companions, who kissed it in turn. When this rite was completed, she took the lead in a round, juggling the glowing bar like a drum major, while the others sang her praises:

> Queen of fires,
> Light the fire!
> Queen of fires,
> Light the fire!
> Light the fire . . .

When finally Marinette stepped out of the fire, Estinval invited her into the *houmfor* to receive the offerings intended for her. With eyes screwed up in an ambiguous smile, both childish and sly, she thanked him, though this was not her custom; but when she saw the food, feigning surprise, she drew herself up and eyed the *houngan* from head to toe.

"If anyone had told me you were dishonest, I wouldn't have believed it!"

"Oh-oh! My friends, just listen to her!" cried Estinval. "I offer her a drink, I offer her food, and she still isn't satisfied!"

"You know very well, hypocrite, that I only eat goats without horns, babies still at the mother's breast."

"And where do you think I can get any for you?"

"That's your problem, Estinval. You propose a deal, I'd like to accept it. But if you think you can pay me as you please, you're greatly mistaken. Besides, I think too much of my *horse* to part with her for the dishonest price you're offering. Such a good mount, who, by the grace of God, has permitted you to earn a fortune . . . I'd kill her instead. . . ."

"We'll see about that!" replied Estinval, turning his back to her.

He went to get Ti-Jean, who was still dancing in the fire with Escalier and Bacoulou.

"Marinette wants to spoil the *service*," he said to him. "Since you're her husband, it's up to you to make her behave."

The *devil* came, very furious, armed with a big whip.

"What's going on here?" he asked menacingly.

Marinette did not answer. Looking stubborn, she glanced at him furtively, with an evil smile.

Ti-Jean was getting impatient. "Woman, it's to you, yes, to you, I'm talking. I want to know what's going on in this house."

"She refuses to touch the food we prepared for her," explained Estinval. "She demands a goat without horns!"

"By thunder!" swore Ti-Jean. "Isn't she disgusting, that woman! If I let her have her way, she'd spend all her time stuffing herself with little babies."

"Why, of course, coward, slave, that's what you say now that you're posing as a respectable man!" she said scornfully. "As though everyone doesn't know it's only your fear of the police that holds you back. Before, when you weren't yet playing civilized, you guzzled so many goats without horns that leprosy hit you, too. Look at his legs, my friends. . . . Ti-Jean Piécheche, that's what they call you sometimes, isn't it?"

"Hell, that's enough out of you!" roared Ti-Jean, snapping his whip. "You'll eat what they give you, or else, may God punish me . . ."

With a leap she bounded out of the room. She bumped against a low chair, fell sprawling, and rolled on the ground in a frenzied disorder of contortions and howls, then raised herself into a backward arc, like a hysteric.

"Quick, grab hold of her!" cried Ti-Jean. "If not, I know the vermin, she could easily break her *horse's* back."

Estinval acted instantly. With the help of his acolytes, he seized her roughly, bound her hands and feet, and then tied her to one of the poles of the *peristyle*. Raising his whip, Ti-Jean applied himself to correcting his intractable spouse. It was not an easy task, because with each lash—while he firmly and patiently exhorted her to accept Estinval's offerings—Marinette hurled gross insults, each more virulent than the last. But, finally exhausted from the flaying, she feigned surrender and ate all that was offered to her. She even assumed the hideous grimace that passed for her smile.

"I have to admit the truth, Estinval. In your house, they know how to cook."

Estinval shrugged his scorn. "That doesn't stop you, Mam'zelle Marinette, from preferring something else. But you must be thirsty now." He walked toward the altar and picked up a bottle of kerosene. "Here," he said. "Thank goodness, we don't lack drinks to welcome you."

She did not hurry to drink. Holding the bottle in her arms and cradling it like a doll, with a wild expression and her voice harsh and sinister, she sang:

> Leaf oh, save my life:
> I'm in misery, oh!
> Leaf oh, save my life:
> I'm in misery, oh!
> My child is sick,
> I run to the *gangan's,* Similor!
> My child is sick,
> I run to the *gangan's,* Similor!

So lugubrious was the chant that a chill gripped the attendants; they remembered the threat Marinette had made against Man Yaya, and, in spite of his courage, Estinval Civilhomme, the protégé of the Masters of the Water, felt his legs weakening.

"Good Lord!" everyone prayed, making the sign of the cross. "Good Lord, our Father!"

But the Good Lord did not seem to hear them, and Marinette, relentless, continued:

> If you're a good *gangan*
> You'll save my life:
> I'm in misery, oh!

Finally she fell silent, uncorked the bottle, and drank calmly, with her eyes closed upon her pleasure.

"Thank you, *gangan*," she said, wiping her mouth with the back of her hand. "Thanks a lot!"

"You're welcome," replied Estinval, his throat tight.

"If you're a good *gangan*, you'll save the life of my *horse*, won't you?"

Thereupon, Marinette burst out laughing sardonically and withdrew from Man Yaya, who fell backwards —stone dead, as they say.

VII

Everything contributed to the ease of the morning as it burst forth in exultation beneath a chalk-blue sky. The bushes cheered up, dazzling with dew, rustled at the tinkle of the anolis' crystaline bello. The mountain was still steaming from the first summer downpour, and already, along its tortured flanks, with wide blood-stained gashes, there grew again an optimistic fur of grass and clover, blooming with dandelions.

The change of scenery had been quite brusque that year. Like a routed army, but dressed in sparkling colors ranging from red through varying shades of yellow to white, for a whole fortnight the butterflies of Midsummer Day had traversed the region from north to south and left behind a few laggards hovering over the pools of water; then, all at once, the weather changed to the chilly season of fog and torrential rains.

Cleansed from the dust of a dry, windy June, Boischandelle warmed itself gently in the sun, while the breeze from the east wafted the fresh smell of resin, fern, and wild strawberries in gusts as it came down from the pine forest, where it had taken on a transparency—with the sparkle and verve that characterize the wines from Champagne.

Rénélus Altidor, however, had no cause to rejoice. For him it was simply the beginning of the rainy season, of a long period of troubles when the highway, frequently soaked, became dangerous and at times even impassable. Thus, the night before, on his way back from Port-au-Prince with a rather heavy load of passengers and merchandise, the Boar of the Mountain went into a skid around the curve at Montjoli. Waiting for help, it had spent a whole hour clinging to the edge of the ravine, holding on only by the front wheels and the weight of the motor. Fortunately, there had been no deaths to mourn, or even any wounded or loss of goods (with the exception, however, of an energetic fighting cock—one of those tough old birds with neck and thighs plucked and rubbed with ginger and pepper—who, panicking from the commotion of the general hullabaloo, had plunged into the abyss in a tumult of wings and screeching), but the accident had upset the inhabitants of the town.

And now, at the regular departure time, despite repeated honkings of the horn, not a single passenger came to board the bus. Most likely, the usual passengers from Boischandelle were loath to travel that day, since they were naturally cautious, and they may very well have sent a messenger to Fonds-Rouge, as they usually did, to ask Estinval the weather forecast for the afternoon. But Rénélus Altidor could not—as he was explaining to his assistant, the *boeuf-chaîne* Ciceron—just hang around with his arms folded, waiting for them. One hour was an hour, and he had to know right away if they were going down to Port-au-Prince or not. He decided to go himself to look for his customers, who lived, for the most part, around the marketplace.

Now, there were crowds of people that day. And, according to custom, the peasant women had set their produce out even into the street, so that no car could risk going through there. Although he was in a hurry, Rénélus Altidor did not have the impatience—as one might be inclined in like circumstances—to interpret this as malice directed against him personally or to get angry at the proverbial lack of discipline of the Haitian people. He simply parked the Boar of the Mountain near the gas station and left it under the vigilant eye of the *boeuf-chaîne* Ciceron. But he had a hard time making his way through the noisy, seething multitude where animals and people, pell-mell, vied for incongruity. So he was streaming with perspiration when he reached the coffee warehouse that belonged to Louis-Jean Février, town councilman and speculator in commodities.

Gloriously indifferent to the hubbub of the common people, his belly rounded between well-spread-out legs, pants legs pulled up—with the double purpose of keeping the crease and showing off his silk hose—Boss Février sat enthroned on the porch in a heavy wool suit of the aristocratic kind called heavy-skin. He was rereading and annotating *The Prince* by Machiavelli, an intellectual recreation in which he indulged from time to time (to relieve the tedium during the off-season, he modestly told his friends, who didn't believe a word of it, knowing well that his enlightened patriotism harbored high ambitions).

Rénélus Altidor touched the brim of his big black felt hat. "Good morning, boss," he said, in a solemn but not obsequious voice.

"Oh-oh! Why, if it isn't Rénélus!" exclaimed Louis-Jean Février gaily, feigning surprise. "How are things, Rénélus?"

Readily interrupting his reading, he closed the book upon his index finger and took off his glasses. "It looks, my good man, like you're not traveling today?"

"I don't know yet, boss. I'm just now checking my customers to know what they've decided."

Louis-Jean Février shook his head and smiled knowingly, but with a touch of compassion. "You haven't heard yet, it seems, that Estinval predicted bad weather for this afternoon."

"Is that so?" sighed Rénélus, bringing his hand to his jaw.

"That's so," said Louis-Jean Février. "And you can be sure we'll get it, that bad weather. You can always count on Estinval, he never makes a mistake! We may well wonder if, when he predicts rain, he doesn't make a deal with the devil to get it to fall. And what looks fishy about it to me is that whenever the water causes damage, he immediately blames my *compère* Josaphat, who isn't involved in magic, much less meteorological forecasts. But the poor man has a broad back; easiest thing in the world to make him the scapegoat. So Estinval never fails to accuse him of being the prime mover of all the bad luck, of all the ills, of all the seasonal disasters that oppress the people of Boischandelle and vicinity. But who gains, who gets rich from the distress of the poor people, if not the *boccor* of Fonds-Rouge, the sinister and powerful father-in-law of Macdonald Origène?"

"You really believe that, boss?" asked Rénélus worriedly.

Then, since Louis-Jean Février didn't seem to catch

what it was all about: "That Estinval can make rain fall at will?"

"And why not, my good man? Isn't Estinval a first-rate magician?"

"But they say he's going to *reject*."

"Yeah!" said Louis-Jean Février. "Last week he held a whole string of *services* to buy off the *loas*. And it all went very well, it seems, except that Marinette almost did poor Man Yaya in, and Estinval had to resuscitate her." He burst out in a frank, hearty laugh, but of short duration—just long enough to show his hilarity.

"What a good joke!" he continued, with tears in his eyes. "Ah! that marvelous thing they call politics . . . But wouldn't it be better if we dropped the subject, Rénélus? We were saying it's going to rain this afternoon and consequently no one will go down to Port-au-Prince. Right? And so your day is free. It happens, too, by chance, that Bellami is at Terre-Froide. So his little goose is home all alone and bored to death. Warning to ladies' men!"

"Han!" said Rénélus with a faint smile as if to say he took the insinuation for a joke, just a bit of teasing based on nothing real. "So Lieutenant is on his rounds."

"On his rounds! Don't you know that terrible things have been happening at Terre-Froide?"

"Oh-oh! oh-oh!" said Rénélus, astonished. "Don't tell me!"

"It concerns, as you might suspect, a new assault by the Soldiers of St. Michael, who are continuing their notorious anti-superstition crusade, encouraged as they are by the benevolent neutrality of the Mayor!" explained Louis-Jean Février. "It seems the little priest went up there with a band of fanatics in tow . . . Madame Origène's clique, let it be said in passing . . .

he preached in Creole and came back down alone, leaving his acolytes at Terre-Froide. To assure the conversion of the inhabitants, he claimed. The fact is, however, that these fellows committed all sorts of crimes in the village, beating the peasants, burning houses, looting, attacking, not only the followers of vodou, but also, and especially, the Protestants . . . and God knows there are plenty of them around there! But to crown it all, under the pretext of baptizing a child who had the whooping cough, they plunged it into the icy waters of the river and the innocent little thing died that night. And that's how, my good man, Bellami had to rush over to the place to reestablish order—if there is still time!"

"Just imagine!" exclaimed Rénélus.

"Isn't it outrageous, really?" said Louis-Jean Février, indignant. Then, going back to his teasing: "But since the ill luck of some is often the good luck of others, it happens, too, that Madame Bellami is all alone today, and you, thanks to Estinval, have involuntary leisure."

Rénélus, embarrassed, scratched the nape of his neck. "Really, boss, I don't see what you're driving at."

"You don't see, my good man! But maybe you'll understand if I tell you that you always remind me of the proverb which says that a good cock crows in all the henhouses."

"You're always kidding, boss. But, as God is my witness, I swear to you on all that is most holy that I've never touched the wife of a friend," the bus driver protested. At the same time he was mindful to press the big toe of his right foot against the ground to nullify his oath.

"Do you expect me to believe that, Rénélus? You're always stuck at poor Bellami's house, especially when he isn't there."

"As far as that's concerned, Boss Février, I won't altogether deny it. Lieutenant is so jealous! But your way of presenting the case has no connection with reality. You see perdition where there is only friendship. Just consider that this Dulce María we're speaking of—the wife of Bellami, but she hadn't yet met him and everyone called her La Paloma—is an old friend of mine, from the time when I was young and frisky and used to go a lot to the Frontier in Port-au-Prince. Besides, the proof that I've never had an affair with her is that she lived like a sister with La Rubia, who had a child from me, as you know."

"Granted, Rénélus. But La Rubia died some years ago, and the child too, and no one is unaware of how hot and lascivious Madame Bellami is. . . . But wouldn't it be better to pick a few leaves and cover up all that?"

Rénélus shrugged. "I guess I'll be going, yes, boss."

Piqued by the plebeian's offhand manner and anxious to mark the distance that separated their social rank—for they were both very black—Boss Février bade him goodbye in a high clear voice. "Goodbye, my good man. That's final, isn't it? The Boar won't be traveling today. . . ."

As he mingled with the crowd in the marketplace, whence rose the occasional squeal of a pig, the mooing of a cow, or the marinated hawking of a woman selling salted fish, Rénélus Altidor suddenly felt his blood boil with anger.

Yes, why didn't Boss Février mind his own business?

"Always ready to stick his nose in other people's business, that one, even when it smells bad!" muttered the driver of the Boar of the Mountain. "You tell me politics has its demands. . . . But, after all, what's it to him whether or not I sleep with Bellami's wife? And then, that way he has of playing people against each other and trying to get you involved in his complicated manipulations. You're a town councilman, and since that seems petty compared to your ambitions, you eye the position of Mayor Origène, until something better shows up. I don't see anything wrong in it, that's the game! He or you, I sort of wonder, what would be the difference for the poor people? You'll become Mayor of Boischandelle, and I'll still be a bus driver. You'll call out to me on the street: 'Rénélus! eh, Rénélus!' and I'll answer respectfully as I walk up to you: 'I beg your pardon, Mr. Mayor.' Then you'll say, 'How are things, my good man?' and I'll grin very gratefully: 'Not bad, Mr. Mayor.' But beyond that, to take me for an idiot and try to make me believe that Estinval can raise the dead back to life and make rain fall at will. No, that's too much! Now Bouqui is in college."

The proverb quickly restored his good humor, and he recalled that for many years now he had quoted it from time to time and the poor legendary idiot had still not succeeded in getting through college. What could he, Rénélus, do about that? And so he drove the Boar of the Mountain to the garage, dismissed his assistant, the *boeuf-chaîne* Ciceron, and left with a light heart as he hummed the popular tune:

Gabélus is a handsome boy.
In his little green pants,
He looks like a parrot . . .

without suspecting that at Bellami's house a rather unpleasant surprise awaited him.

64

VIII

We know that before she began to live with Lieutenant Charles-Oscar Bellami and then married him before God and man, Dulce María Gómez y Rosas, called La Paloma, had lived for several years at the Frontier, in the brothel district of Port-au-Prince, that midway of sordid pleasures, at once sad and rotten, which clustered its bars and *dancings* around the southern end of the Grand-Rue and owed its name to the Dominican colony —prostitutes, pimps, homosexuals, brothelkeepers, and other merchants of slow death, which held, so to speak, the highest status there.

The subtle demon of *bovarysme* had taken her there.

She was born on the shores of Lake Enriquillo in the town of La Descubierta, where her father was a cobbler, and since childhood she had nursed the romantic ambition of going to live in Santo Domingo. Two of her aunts were working there as seamstresses, or so they claimed; but, as the photographs showed, they dressed elegantly—at least, so it seemed to the inhabitants of the town—and all the members of the family were proud of it, except the father, who was of a suspicious and surly nature.

At the age of sixteen, on the strength of these photographs, Dulce María eloped with a young officer who was going to the capital. She did not find her aunts, who had recently left, she was told, for the Haitian city of Gonaïves, where a squadron of the United States Navy put into port during the course of maneuvers. And soon, surely taken up with a new idyll, the heaven-sent seducer abandoned her to her fate without as much as a goodbye. He left her with about ten dollars, just enough to pay the cheap rent and return to La Descubierta, where doubtless some harsh punishment was in store for her. She did not go back home, not because she feared her father's brutality, for she was used to being beaten, but because she had no intention of giving up the fascinating spectacle of the big city, the rather vague ideal she called *lo bello* and which she felt was the very essence of living.

Pleasingly rounded, as though turned on a lathe, with the freshness and tenderness of a peach, it was easy for her to fall into vice. Already from a distance, by clear signs, it seemed terribly inviting, and promised her a pleasant, bold, and lucrative career.

She started out proud, earned a good living, and saved nothing, but showed perseverance, and one fine morning after various adventures that took her to different countries, the Greater as well as the Lesser Antilles, she rented a room at the Marine Bar in Port-au-Prince, the most prosperous of the *dancings* of the Frontier, where, thanks to the American occupation troops, the "Spanish girls" were then in great demand: they came from different countries of the hemisphere, from Barcelona, too . . . and even from Marseilles!

Despite the recurring exhaustion of venal love, the beer, the late hours every day, La Paloma was no less attractive than when she first started. She had acquired experience along the way, and her flesh, still firm, seemed to be seasoned by it. The cooing inflections of her voice had more suppleness, more depth, a more convincing warmth; her golden quadroon face and her burning innocent eyes infallibly lured the serious customer. So, in his turn, Ramírez, the owner of the brothel —a former cowhand from Cibao whom his fellow countrymen, enthusiastic over his success, honored by the extravagant nickname of *el Indio,* though his obvious negritude had been spared any mixing—was caught like a young man. First he made her his protégée, then took her out of circulation, as they say.

From then on she reigned at the cash register near the end of the counter, where her numerous former clients, reduced to lustful glances, would come, one after the other—or in small groups on affluent days—to have a consoling drink with her, which they paid for wholeheartedly in hopes that some day . . . sometime when Ramírez . . . and other hints of the same intensity, which they were careful not to articulate but eloquently expressed by a look, a gradation of sighs, or a reticent word of praise.

Meanwhile, the Indian covered La Paloma with jewels, bought her a brand-new Cadillac, and kept an eye on her day and night without letup.

Although he was a strong fellow of good height with a scarred face, Ramírez was not quarrelsome, even when drunk—which happened rarely—but he was not afraid of a fight or of keeping his hand in when some bully seemed to deserve a little attention, and since he was known for his accuracy in wielding a knife, he did not have much trouble.

Two years passed thus in the monotony of the milieu, the rigid routine of conventional pleasures, while the loudspeakers blared out stupefying music—all the Afro-American rhythms, from blues to rhumbas, going through the beguines and calypsos, in relentless, continuous, obsessive succession. And as one does in pain or the satisfaction of a call of nature, Ramírez had a feeling of infinity, so that in the long run, since his business kept on prospering, it seemed to him that it would last forever.

Hence, when the Marines left, instead of attributing the phenomenon to the objective action of a law of nature—that everything comes to an end, for example—he chalked it up to his bad luck. In fact, you would have thought that practical life was contriving to provide solid reasons to support his point of view; from one day to the next, his receipts fell to the level of his slowest evenings, and little by little, to hold out as he waited for a providential reversal of the situation, he was obliged to sell the Cadillac, then La Paloma's jewels—in short, to divest himself of the most tangible symbols of his prosperity.

And that was not all, for, as materialists have observed, facts are hardheaded; once they have started in a chosen direction, you cannot pull them back, even if you tug by the tail. Notwithstanding the enticing promises he made to the Black Virgin of Higüey and other more or less absurd entreaties (every morning, in order to rout his bad luck, he sprinkled the doors of the brothel with a repulsing mixture of rotten urine and asafetida, then lit a candle in front of the miraculous image of the Altagracia), Ramírez's boarders left the country for the most part, emigrating in doubtful quest of a better life.

He was reduced to taking on Haitian whores, whom he scorned because of their relative modesty, quite comical after all, since it came directly from bourgeois ideas which were completely out of place in the establishment. They would not have agreed to take off their slips for anything in the world. And their indolence in the work of the profession being comparable to the proverbial laziness of the lizard, he thought of them somewhat as cold-blooded animals—hadn't one client, hurt in his male pride, publicly revealed that at the height of the sexual act the chosen bitch had said to him in straight raw terms to hurry up and finish? Consequently, the Indian boosted the personnel with three Frenchwomen, rather past their prime; one, a querulous drunkard, had already lost all her incisors from the intensive use of mercury. But since, after all, they were white . . .

Meantime, the decline continued.

Being in debt to his suppliers as well as the owner of the house, he was forced to sell off part of the furnishings and set himself up in smaller quarters. But as the decline worsened, the primitive violence of his character, irritated by the progressive abuse of liquor, came to the fore, and this led to his exhausting La Paloma with his sexual demands and beating her more often than was reasonable, so that finally, one evening, overcome with fatigue, she too expressed the intention of leaving him.

"*¿Que me importa que tu me dejes? ¡Estoy cansado de ti!*" he declared in a voice full of hatred, as he walked toward the bar.

Quickly she went to pack her bags.

Ramírez shrugged and swallowed about ten glasses of

rum in quick succession. He had been expecting this for quite some time without admitting it to himself, and even now he was trying to persuade himself the break was not possible, that Dulce María was too attached to him sensually to leave him. In any case, he told himself, whether she left or not, he didn't give a damn! One less responsibility, after all. And then, isn't it a fact, for each one lost . . . ?

But when La Paloma came out of her room looking for a porter, he said to her rudely: *"¡Ven aquí, puta sucia! ¿Adonde vas?"*

Since she did not stop, he hurled a bottle of soda at her head, which just missed her and smashed against one of the columns of the porch.

"¡Carajo!" he said, pulling a razor out of his pocket.

He dashed after her, but she was already in the street and running as fast as she could toward the police station at Portail Léogane, which fortunately was close by.

"¡Venga!" he screamed in a raucous voice, trembling with grotesque rage and already out of breath. *"Ven, que te corto la garganta . . ."*

This is how Bellami, alerted by the Indian's screams, entered the life of Dulce María Gómez y Rosas. It happened that Ramírez had been involved in the cocaine trade during the American occupation and still had a certain quantity left. La Paloma revealed its hiding place to her savior; Ramírez was condemned to prison, then deported.

A little later, as a reward for his exploit, Bellami, then an officer candidate, was promoted to the rank of second lieutenant. Everything seemed to promise rapid advancement, for he was rough enough to merit it. (And he doubtless could have got it if later on—believing he had got his hands on the father of dialectical

materialism, whom the then President had just de-
nounced in a resounding speech—he had not created a
diplomatic incident by arresting a certain Dr. Karl
Marx, an agent of the Third Reich on his way to Ciudad
Trujillo as Director of the Dominican-German Insti-
tute. At least, he would not have been relegated to
Boischandelle.) As far as La Paloma was concerned, she
had simply gone full circle round. A military man had
led her into prostitution; another was getting her out
of it.

IX

Gabélus, come back and kiss me.
Come back!
Come back!
Come back and give me a sweet caress . . .

"Yes, why doesn't Boss Février mind his own business?" repeated Rénélus Altidor, but this time he was smiling with good humor.

He was approaching Charles-Oscar Bellami's house, and lustful memories stronger than his rancor beset him from all sides. With the fond intent of crying "Cuckoo, here he is," he gently pushed the lattice door, walked through the living room on tiptoe, then the dining room, and surprised the cooing Paloma, completely naked in her bed, simperingly chatting with Alcius, Madame Origène's godchild. It's true that the boy, standing in the middle of the room, had all his clothes on and was modestly lowering his eyes, visibly embarrassed by the situation; but the driver of the Boar of the Mountain did not take the thing lightly.

"That's all we needed!" he stated angrily. "Now

you're robbing the cradle. And besides, look who we have here! A servant, a little *resté-avec—*"

"*Dios mío,* Rénéliss!"

"—but since the gentleman is reputed to be virgin and especially to have one of those tools—"

"Oh, my God, Rénéliss!"

"—a veritable table leg, as they say . . ."

The fact is that a neighbor, with a hairy chin but quite sensitive, as she opened her window early in the morning on Midsummer Day had seen Alcius, naked as Adam, washing himself in the Origène backyard, and she had been so upset by her discovery that she couldn't keep from telling her friends, who, in turn . . .

"Shameless as I know you are," continued Rénélus Altidor, "you certainly wanted to be the first . . ."

"Eet ees no true, no, *papacito mío!*" protested Dulce María in her most disingenuous way, pulling the sheet over her. "No true at all. Alciis 'ave bring to me two botell of rhun that Lieutenant 'ad order fron the Señora de Oridgène. *Aquí están, sobre la mesa.* . . . *Y yo* 'ave djus geeve heem the money when you enter, *chico.* . . ."

"Yeah," said Rénélus, crossing his arms in the implacable attitude of an executioner. "And that's just why you took off all your clothes, isn't it?"

"I'll be going, yes, Madame Bellami," ventured Alcius timidly.

"You stay right there!" ordered the bus driver sternly. "Show me the money."

Alcius opened his hand. "Here it is, yes, boss."

"All right, you can go back to your master's now. But don't ever let me catch you in this house again."

"Thanks, yes, boss."

"Thanks! Thanks, what?" yelled the bus driver.

"Listen, you dirty little insect, you'd just better leave unless you want me to twist your neck and pull off your head like a chicken."

Alcius didn't wait to be told twice, and once in the street, he gave in to panic and fled like a thief.

Then, slowly, with the patient cruelty of a torturer, Rénélus Altidor walked toward the bed, where Madame Bellami, huddled up like a submissive cat, was already sobbing with anguish and desire.

"Now, for the two of us," he said.

He took off his jacket, put it on a chair, and rolled up his shirtsleeves. Then he took off his belt and, holding it by the buckle, anchored it firmly with two turns around his fist, then pulled back the covers with a brutal gesture and started the punishment.

"If Bellami can't soften you up," he cried as he struck her, "if he can't tame you . . . well, then . . . I, as my name is Rénélus Altidor . . . I'll do him this favor . . . I'll break you in. . . ."

He lashed at her body methodically, bruising her breasts, her belly, and legs in turn, not even sparing her face. And Madame Bellami, her nostrils dilated as she made cooing sounds, was writhing with pleasure. *"Ay, papacito . . . ay . . . ay . . . que terrible tú eres . . . yes . . . yes . . ."*

"I'll quench the heat in your blood. . . . I'll break your bones. . . . I'll make you quit those bad Spanish cat habits . . . that dirty prostitute's trade. . . . I'll make you . . ."

"Yes . . . you're right. . . . *Mátame, hombre, mátame . . . Yo . . . yo . . ."*

"I'll make you stop those whore habits!"

"*Yo* ask you to do eet. . . . *Ay, papacito, como* you beat me well . . . *como* you love me!"

At these words, Rénélus's fury reached the limit. He brusquely threw the belt to the floor and seized Madame Bellami by the throat.

"Ah, I love you?" he roared like a madman. "You say I love you? Well, may God punish me, Dulce María, if I don't strangle you this morning!"

Suddenly she saw murder in his eyes; her mouth sprang wide open and she uttered a great mute cry. Rénélus was already sinking his fingers in around her larynx as if to pull it out with her whole voice—that voice so cherished, whose most sincere and intimate moans he had known—when the lattice door opened noisily and the Angel's trumpet was heard like a clap of thunder above the darkness of insanity.

"What is this Capernaum in the home of an absentee legionary?"

Fortunately, it was only the Justice of the Peace. He lived across the street, and hearing angry voices, he thought it might be a dangerous family quarrel and was chivalrously rushing to the aid of feminine frailty.

"What do I see, great God!" he exclaimed at the door of the bedroom, speechless at the spectacle unfolding before his stern eyes.

He had naïvely believed it was Lieutenant Bellami, and now, look. . . .

"But, but, but . . . are we, my friends, in Babylon?" he wondered with an anxiety that grew to panic proportions, and he was looking at all the walls around the room to see if some mysterious hand had not written the prophetic *mene, mene, tekel, upharsin*. Fortunately, the famous threat was not there.

And as Rénélus was straightening out his clothes, more annoyed than embarrassed, but with a cynical grin, Septimus Morency was suddenly filled with the bitterness of Jeremiah.

"O heavens! O misfortune!" he cried, lifting his arms to call on God as witness. "The noble city of Boischandelle is co-rrupted! A wolf! a hoodlum! a lycanthrope! has fraudulently stolen into the Centurion's sheepfold!"

Then, with a sudden spurt of energy, his eyes shut: "Rénélus Altidor," he said, pointing toward the door, "pick up your things and get the hell out of here!"

The driver of the Boar of the Mountain remembered Alcius and was amused at the similarity of the situations, for, while they seemed alike, among other things the roles were not the same. This time it was the intruder giving orders to clear out to the one who had a right to be there.

"Thanks, Mr. Justice," he said, with mocking obsequiousness. "Thanks very much."

He bowed, touched the brim of his felt hat, but did not leave. And the Justice of the Peace shrugged, understanding the malicious insinuation Rénélus's attitude implied. He could think all he wanted, that car-driving whosis, everybody knew the moral rectitude of Septimus Morency, didn't they?

Meanwhile, with her face buried in the pillows and her body shaken by convulsive shudders, Madame Bellami wept silently. Finally noticing her shameless attire, the Justice of the Peace picked up her dressing gown where it trailed on the floor and handed it to her with eyes averted in a show of modesty, though he was quite sincere.

"Hide from me, madame," he said, "hide from me that nudity that I must not see."

Besides, it was starting to get cold.

From the nearby mountain passes, where it had been

continuously lifting, gently creeping along the gullied slopes fragrant with herbs, the fog was filtering into the house in successive puffs as the deceptive sound of the pine trees suggested the nearness of the sea, that "maternal comforter of the suffering."

But just as the sun was clouding over—for greater harmony, discretion, and peace, it seemed—a horse trotted into the yard and abruptly halted.

"Han!" said Rénélus Altidor, sneering. "If I'm not mistaken, here's Lieutenant!"

The Justice of the Peace stared fixedly; he was about to lose his head.

"Quick, dear friend," he implored in everyday language, "clear out quick or Bellami might do something rash!"

"Something rash, Mr. Justice? Don't you think, rather, that if he found you alone with his wife in her present state . . ."

"How's that?" asked Septimus, getting on his high horse. "And for what, by chance, would I be justiciable?"

"My presence saves you, on the contrary, Mr. Justice," Rénélus continued seriously, "for you don't know what happened before you came. Let me handle this and you'll see that everything will end well for everyone. Only, don't say anything except to support me, if I need it."

"*Alea jacta est!*" sighed the Justice of the Peace, regaining his Latin.

And, in fact, the bus driver's boldness cleared up the situation. To the indignant surprise of Septimus Morency, who, in spite of himself, felt coerced into the humiliating role of accomplice, Rénélus gave a clever and false version of the facts, which got him out of a tight spot and also permitted him to avenge himself on Alcius, whom, justly or not, he considered a rival. He explained that the latter had attempted rape on the person of Madame Bellami, and that he, Rénélus, happening by, had heard the cries of the victim and rushed to her aid, but that the aggressor had had time to get away through a window. When he saw this, he called the Justice of the Peace to report the matter.

Bellami did not wait to hear more. He ran to the yard, mounted his horse, and rode full tilt to the home of Macdonald Origène, whom he found in the living room knotting his bow tie and ready to leave for the town hall.

"Where is that scoundrel Alcius?" he asked bluntly, without as much as a greeting. "I've come to arrest him."

The Mayor of Boischandelle stopped "scrutinizing" in the oval mirror the "specific" effects of his iridescent tie, turned around slowly, with all the dignity the situation called for, and presented to the officer his most severe mask.

"Oh, pardon, Mayor Origène!" said the latter, embarrassed. "I didn't mean to be impolite, no. But you know, when someone is angry . . ."

Instinctively he stood at attention and brought his hand up to the visor of his kepi. "Good morning, Mr. Mayor."

"Good morning, whosis . . . uh . . . uh . . . isn't it . . . Lieutenant Bellami."

In the next room, where she had her grocery store— the most important one in Boischandelle—Madame Origène sat comfortably in a wicker armchair holding an aluminum pan between her imposing thighs and shelling fresh peas for the midday meal. She interrupted her task and with impassive face put the receptacle down beside her and rose majestically from her rustic seat.

"If you please, Mayor Origène," asked Bellami timidly, "is Alcius here?"

"That is to say . . . Alcius . . . yes, I believe he's here," answered the Mayor.

Visibly annoyed, he called his wife, as he always did in conflicts concerning servants, which he did not consider within his jurisdiction: "Madame Origène!"

She was already standing in the doorway, her hands behind her back and a hostile look on her face.

"Good morning, Lieutenant," she said coldly. "I heard you say you came to arrest my godchild. I'd like to know why."

"This morning," he said in a quavering voice, "Alcius tried to rape Madame Bellami."

"Alcius, yes, Lieutenant? A quiet boy who is still growing and would have become a Protestant if I had not been against it? But, of course, since you tell me . . ." She shook her head to emphasize her disbelief. "I'm curious, however, to know what could have pushed him into acting like Cadet Jacques."

"It was Rénélus, yes, who reported it to me . . . in the very presence of the Justice of the Peace."

"Rénélus Altidor, did you say? The one I know?"

"The very same."

"You may go on with your story, Lieutenant."

Bellami lowered his eyes under Madame Origène's ironic gaze. "Rénélus was walking past our house this morning when he heard my wife's cries. Being an old friend, he went in to see what was the matter. But just then Alcius got away through the window. Septimus arrived a moment later. And I found them both in the

79

bedroom trying to calm poor Dulce María, who was almost hysterical and couldn't stop sobbing."

"And what does Sèpe say about all that?"

"Sèpe!" said the officer, looking at the ceiling. "Sèpe . . . he didn't say anything, since he arrived after the attack. Alcius had already disappeared."

"Ah-ha!" said Madame Origène, her nostrils triumphant. "And Madame Bellami herself?"

"Madame Bellami . . . but she couldn't talk at all, because of the state she was in."

"And so, if I understand correctly, you didn't question them?"

"No," he tried to explain, "I didn't have the time. . . . I saw red, and . . ."

"Well, my friend, go and question them right now. For my part, I'll attend to Alcius. If he's guilty, I'll see it right away and I'll send for you to come and arrest him. If he isn't, we'll forget the whole thing and not mention it again. Is that clear, Lieutenant?"

Poor Bellami was so ashamed he didn't know which foot to move forward in order to get away.

"By the way," added Madame Origène pitilessly, "if you'll permit me to give you a little advice, I'll tell you that if I were you, I wouldn't allow Rénélus access to my house. He's not someone you should be friendly with, much less your wife. . . ."

All it cost La Paloma was another whipping. But she defended herself like a tigress this time, scarring her husband's face all over with deep scratches. And, as usual, the fight between husband and wife ended in wild embraces. But the incident, quickly making the rounds, had unfortunate consequences for Alcius.

For some time, we recall, he had loved Hortense Joseph, the daughter of the *houngan* from Bassin-Bleu, who, like him, frequented the church of the Pentecostalists. And naturally, the two adolescents planned to marry as soon as they were old enough and could afford it. They had not mentioned it to anyone, and their closeness had not awakened the interest of the scandalmongers. But after the adventure of La Paloma, their relationship became the object of venomous gossip, representing the chaste Alcius as an intrepid satyr with an enormous penis. Quite soon it reached the ears of Josaphat, who already, in his hatred of anyone connected distantly or closely with Estinval, was inclined to believe the story of the attempted rape. Determined not to have his daughter marry a servant—who to top it all, as he said indignantly, was the *resté-avec* of a Civilhomme—he forbade Hortense not only to see Alcius but also to attend religious services at the Protestant church.

X

A spirit of great excitement filled the air that evening at Bassin-Bleu. Uneasy about the growing boldness of the Soldiers of St. Michael, and especially about the conversion of Estinval, who was going to *reject* the next morning together with his confraternity, Josaphat Joseph had assembled the rank and file of the vodou society called Trésor des Nagos, of which he was life president.

Officially, it was supposed to be only an entertainment, a simple dance, as they say, and it was for this purpose, moreover, that the meeting—like the *services* held previously by his rival at Fonds-Rouge—had been permitted by Lieutenant Bellami, who otherwise would have forbidden it; but, in reality, its purpose was to hold propitiatory rites, to evoke the principal *mystères* of the Arada cult, to get their advice on how to conduct themselves during the religious conflict that was disturbing the region, and finally, to offer a sacrifice to the Master of the House, the powerful Ogou Ferraille, god of war and fire.

The weather looked favorable for the ceremony.

About midday, a violent shower had washed the mountain as though to purify it, then the clouds, like an immense herd of buffaloes, had migrated toward the sea, where the sun was now going down in a riot of blood and fire, splashing the surrounding heights, so that everything seemed to contribute to the apotheosis of the great *mystère* Nago.

As the guests arrived—and they were coming from all the neighboring communities: from Pays-Sec, from Trois-Pins, from the town of Boischandelle, from Bellefontaine, and even from Fonds-Rouge, where Estinval thought he ruled without competition—the excitement in the enclosure mounted. The fact was that Josaphat, past master at advertising, carefully nurtured his reputation as a generous host. And this time, as he did for important occasions, he had set up bars around the *peristyle* as well as game tables. Moreover, the rumor spread, passed along by the members of the Society of the Trésor des Nagos, that he had had a steer slaughtered, three castrated pigs, ten goats, and to top it off, that Boss Février, the town councilman, had sent him as a gift two barrels of clairin and five gallons of rum—the wherewithal for feasting from Saturday afternoon to Monday's dawn.

All was ablaze that evening. Bodies and souls glowed in concert with the sky and mountain. And since red is the color of Ogou Ferraille, patron of warriors and ironsmiths, the temple and courtyard were decked out in it; also, the members of Josaphat's confraternity had worn for the occasion red blouses, jackets, or kerchiefs as a symbol of blood and fire.

Electrified by the staccato beat of the *hogan,* which by itself sounded like an entire steel works, and supported by the powerful choir of the *hounsis-bossales,* the trio of conical drums was beating out an infernal rhythm under the *peristyle,* drawing the *hounsis-canzos* into an obsessive round, strong and precise, circling the *poteau-mitan* on which hung red lanterns and bouquets of scarlet flowers.

Everything was ablaze at Bassin-Bleu.

Already, during the course of successive possessions, the great gods of the Arada pantheon had come down among the faithful—among others, Atibon Legba, Grandmother Ayizan, Papa Loko, Master Agoué, Agaou-Tonnerre, Mistress Erzilie Fréda Dahomey, Minister Azaca Médé, Ayida and Dambala Ouèdo—and all of them had expressed their anger at the hostile acts of the Catholic clergy and had advised the vodou followers to put up the most obstinate resistance. One of them, Sim'bi the healer, had even made a veiled allusion to Estinval Civilhomme.

"I am from the nation of the Congos," he had said. "After leaving Guinea with your ancestors, I suffered greatly because the Creole Negroes were not grateful for all we were doing for them. At that time, except for the Three Kings, there were no other doctors on earth. The leaf doctors today go into the woods, gather simples, and do a good business. But before them, we alone had the power to heal the sick. . . . They say it is the Masters of the Water who trained them, and that we are demons; we do not defend ourselves. You have deceived us but you cannot ever drop us, because the Congos alone do good. They are the Negroes from Africa, they are not mixed. They live under a big rock in deep water. And we renew that water every seven years. . . . My children, it is in parables, yes, that I speak to you tonight. I have my reasons for it. But so much the worse for you if you break away from us! So much the worse for you!"

Agassou Djémen, by contrast, making a brief summary of the situation, used more direct, virile language.

"They claim that all the *mystères* are maleficent spirits," the crab god had said. "It is not true, my friends. We, too, are the children of the Good Lord. It is He Himself, in person, who made us with His own hands. And if He created us, angels and saints, it was so we could take care of the complicated affairs of men, because He Himself, poor devil, is too old for that. I have to tell you, too, that you've disgusted Him with your jealousies, your wild ambitions, and all your intrigues. We are sometimes accused of doing evil. But tell me, my friends, who's to blame? If you charm us by magic, if you trap us by your alluring promises with your beautiful words, what can we do? You pay me to do evil, I do it, and I am not more responsible for it than you. I'm doing my work as a *loa,* for I have to earn my living. But if you have good intentions and your desires are honest, and if you serve me in a way that satisfies me, there is nothing I would not do for your welfare. Now, I've heard that the Catholic priests are all mad, that they have been unleashed and set against us. But these priests are mere human beings, and human beings are not the Good Lord. On the contrary, all of them should serve us. But instead they have taken up arms against us, and they want to overthrow our government. . . . Ayayaye! my friends, so much the worse for them, so much the worse for Mr. Estinval and his followers. Before long, they'll bite their thumbs till they draw blood. We are stronger than they are because it's the Good Lord who entrusted us with our mission on the earth. And none other can take that power away from us. I have spoken, yes, my friends, and I hope you have all heard me. Now I have to leave you. I am going. . . ."

Now it was the turn of the Master of the House.

With a mixture of wheat flour and ashes, which he took from a bowl between thumb and index finger, Josaphat sketched on the ground the *vèvè* depicting the warlike attributes of the *mystère* Nago. As he was performing this rite—the principal act of any evocation—the *reine-chanterelle* started the following hymn, which was soon taken up by the choir:

> Ogou oh, Ferraille oh,
> Come to our aid.
> I say: Ogou oh, Ferraille oh,
> Come to our aid.
> I hear the cannon,
> I hear the guns.
> But you are a man of war.
> Ogou oh, Ferraille oh,
> Come to our aid.
> I say: Ogou oh, Ferraille oh,
> Come to our aid. . . .

Having finished the magic design, Josaphat sprayed it with a generous libation of rum, the god's favorite beverage. Then he sprinkled gunpowder over it and set fire to it, producing a great flame. And as the singers, the *hogantier,* and the drummers became more spirited, compelling, imperious, he gave the invocation in a guttural voice, all the while shaking the little bell and the *asson.*

"General Ogou oh, man of war, man of politics, we are in danger. The Catholic priests want to persecute us.

86

But you are the Master of the House. You must come to the aid of your children and take the whole family under your protection. I am calling General Ogou oh, man of politics, man of war!"

The General, who was always sumptuously received at Bassin-Bleu, was quite cooperative. He immediately mounted his favorite *horse*, none other than Dieudonné, the youngest of Josaphat's sons and his appointed successor. An adolescent of about fifteen, he looked no older than twelve because he was short and sickly. But his sullen face, his little shifty eyes, always bloodshot, gave him a malevolent air, at once cruel and mean. He limped, too, like Toussaint L'Ouverture, and for this reason Boss Février, his affectionate godfather, had bestowed on him the nickname Fatras-Bâton, unkindly given to the "Precursor" in his childhood. And since he was already a high-ranking initiate, the weight of the *mystère* did not floor him. He only staggered a little and was immediately supported by his father, who gathered him tenderly in his arms and wiped his face with a large red handkerchief.

Night had fallen meantime, and with velvet tread scattered along the country a fresh smell of spring water and humus, fragrant with sweet basil. From all around, the whistling frogs were already calling to each other in the depths of the fog, which was getting thicker, inviting to love and relaxation. But the violent nature of Ogou Ferraille, whose personality brutally pushed that of the possessed one into the limbo of unconsciousness, was quick to assert itself. Leaping up suddenly, the god took hold of the sword provided for him where it was stuck into the packed earth of the *peristyle* near the *poteau-mitan*.

"It's me, eh!" he said, drawing himself up proudly.

"It's me, Ogou Ferraille. I heard you calling me for help. Dahomey agrees to it. Here I am, family! Here I am, children!"

He set the point of the sword against his belly, and pressing against it as though to push it into his bowels, he bent the blade into a half-circle, to show that he was invulnerable. Then, without warning, he attacked Josaphat; but, anticipating the assault, which was part of the ceremonial, the *houngan* had already armed himself with a machete. There ensued a rather lively fight, more or less staged, after which the *mystère,* acknowledging the courage and skill of his priest, shook his hands and congratulated him warmly.

"Just look at that!" he said gallantly to Josaphat. "You're a real man, and by God's grace, the one is not yet born who could find a chink in your armor."

The drummers quickly beat the general salute, for the moment had come to render the honors due him as a general. Next, one after the other, the initiates came to prostrate themselves at his feet for the ritual salute, and taking hold of a hand, Ogou made each of them get up and three times made them turn around—to the right, then to the left, and again to the right—and at the end of each turn, each one bowed together with the *mystère.*

Finally, they led the latter into the *houmfor,* and as they solemnly dressed him in his warrior's trappings, the enthusiastic choir of the *hounsis-bossales* celebrated his valor in a hymn repeated at length without the slightest lapse or the least variation:

> Ogou oh, Ferraille oh!
> Come with me.
> I say: Ogou oh, Ferraille oh!
> Come with me.

The cannon can roar,
The guns can fire.
Pay no attention.
Come with me.
Ogou oh, Ferraille oh!
Come with me.
I say: Ogou oh, Ferraille oh!
Come with me. . . .

He came back rigged out as a general of the old army: blue dolman, madder-red trousers, riding boots, the whole topped off with a plumed cocked hat of the picturesque type that in the good old days of Haitian militarism was commonly called *retapé*. Originally, from all appearances, this cheap finery had assured the prestige of a hero of modest, if not middling, proportions; but the different parts of the uniform had to be shortened and taken in at the sides to adjust them to Dieudonné's size, and the boots and hat had simply been stuffed with paper. So the *mystère*, for all his glorious airs, achieved some unexpected effects—quite grotesque, to tell the truth.

But no one noticed.

And when Ogou Ferraille sat on an improvised throne—a straw-bottomed armchair draped in scarlet for the occasion—it was with the utmost respect that they gave him to kiss the society's banners (one of which was the colors of the national flag, blue and red . . . or rather, his own colors, since he had also adopted them). Finally, after gulping down a whole bottle of rum, then lighting a big Havana cigar, he deigned to honor the assembly with a sweeping glance around the room, pretending astonishment, as though he just then had become aware of their presence.

"Ladies and gentlemen, the company, good evening!" he said, pensively.

"Good evening, Papa, good evening!" they answered.

"Are all the *pitites-caille* assembled?"

"Yes, Papa."

He counted the initiates with his finger, and as though they seemed less than expected, he counted them again and shook his head.

"Family!" he said, with increasing concern.

"Beg your pardon, Papa?"

"How many times have you answered me?"

"Once, yes, Papa."

After a moment of meditation, Ogou repeated between puffs: "Family!"

"Beg your pardon, Papa?"

"How many times have you answered me?"

"Twice, yes, Papa."

Ogou did not seem satisfied. He tried again: "Family!"

"Beg your pardon, Papa?"

"How many times have you answered me?"

"Three times, Papa."

Then, still looking worried, Ogou Ferraille got up with his hands clasped behind his back and paced the floor.

"My children!" he said finally and stood still. "If I speak to you now, will you listen to me?"

"That's just why we are here," replied Josaphat.

"I know it very well. But after all these fine speeches you've heard, you must be tired."

"No, Papa, we're not tired."

"I don't want to say anything bad about the *mystères* who preceded me tonight. No. Only, I have to make a little remark; those people like to talk too much. I will not do the same. Besides, you know me; my speeches are always the noise of the cannon, of rifles and machine guns. However, to be fair, I have to acknowledge that what the other *loas* said to you a while ago is good advice, yes. But, after all, they didn't tell you anything you didn't already know. But so that you won't let yourselves be taken by surprise as the inhabitants of Terre-Froide did last week, I came to announce to you that the enemy will attack you right here, no later than tomorrow."

"Right here, General Ogou!" cried Josaphat, unbelieving. "In your own house!"

"Right here! And the fight will be terrible. You'll get some bad blows. There will be bloodshed, there will be fire. But whatever happens, hold out, don't give up. You'll win in the end. And it's me, Ogou Ferraille, man of war, man of politics, telling you. The little priest, ayayaye! because he's French, he thinks he is stronger than we are. It seems he has forgotten that it's our job to make war against the whites, that we have already defeated and chased their ancestors out of this country. So we have to refresh their memory."

"You said it, Papa Ogou!" approved Josaphat, smiling.

And the congregation, enthusiastic, cried: "You said it!"

"*Lan-mitan!*" said Ogou, addressing his priest.

"Beg your pardon, Papa?"

"Do you know what I've decided?"

"No, Papa."

"Oh-oh, you don't know! But it's what you all want. I've decided not to leave tonight and to stay with you until the end of the battle, when the enemy will be defeated and routed."

"Oh, thank you, Papa, thanks a lot!" said Josaphat, full of joy.

Then, addressing the faithful: "My friends, I don't understand you, no! What are you waiting for to shout: 'Vive General Ogou'?"

The acclamations rose in a sudden burst, fused into a single spray, lifted to the stars, and then drifted down again like fireworks. Finally, the choir resumed singing the praises of Ogou Ferraille, and the drums woke up again, spurred on by the *hogan*.

And they danced until daybreak.

XI

About six o'clock, headed by Estinval, whose imperious goatee quivered in the morning breeze, the peasants from the rural section of Fonds-Rouge (except, of course, the dissenters, members of the confraternity of Josaphat Joseph, who had taken no part in the liberation rites) had all gathered at the church of Boischandelle. The sly old man had not bragged to his son-in-law; he really did have complete control of his clients, for not one of them had failed to answer his call. All of them, however, ill at ease in their Sunday clothes, had a blank expression and unsteady step.

Shaken by a supernatural dread at the thought of the impending renunciation of the faith of their ancestors, which was being represented to them as a camouflaged form of Satanism, they attended the Mass in a state close to stupor that went from bad to worse until the moment came to take the pledge they both feared and desired, so that they looked like a veritable troop of *zombis,* of bodies emptied of spiritual substance, each kneeling in turn before the priest. They were remembering, too, that Man Yaya, since her "death" and "resurrection," kept on raving.

93

Since not one of them could read, they repeated—one group of words after the other, and not without mangling them—the oath that the sacristan dictated:

"I, before God present in the tabernacle, before the priest representing Him, renew the promises of my Baptism. With my hand on the Gospel, I swear that I will never give any *manger-loa* whatever, I will never attend any vodou ceremony whatever, I will never take part in any *service-loa* of any kind whatever.

"I swear that I will have destroyed or myself destroy, as soon as possible, all the fetishes and objects of superstition, if there are any, on my person, in my house, in my habitation. . . ."

As none of the things they had most feared happened (crises of possession, mental alienation, or sudden death), they quietly filed out of the church, transfigured, and joined the faithful in the marketplace, where the procession was forming which was to go to Estinval Civilhomme's house so as to give more glamour and prestige to the exorcism of his property. Father Le Bellec, clad in a surplice and purple stole, holding a crucifix in his hands, finally took the lead, and it got under way at once as the sacristan set the bells loudly pealing and the Children of Mary and the Ladies of the Third Order sang in unison with listless voice:

> We want God, Virgin Mary,
> Lend your ear to our plea.
> We implore you, Mother dear,
> Come to the aid of your children. . . .

The procession was entering the Grand-Rue when the Soldiers of St. Michael, who until then had not joined in the thin, inane chorus of the devout women, took up the refrain with all the masculine vigor they could muster—that is to say, at the top of their lungs:

Hear, oh tender Mother,
This cry of our faith:
We want God, He is our Father.
We want God, He is our King.

There was no one in the streets, and all the doors were closed, for, with the exception of the authorities, who were concerned lest they displease the government, the whole town was taking part in the priest's pious venture. Hence the porches were decorated with bouquets of flowers attached to the columns; and rugs, multicolored lengths of cloth, and curtains were hung from the balconies and windows of storied houses.

When they came to the entrance of the Garde d'Haiti post, a squad of soldiers under the command of Sergeant Fortuné joined the procession. Father Le Bellec was surprised not to see Bellami at the head of his men; he asked the reason and the subordinate answered that on Friday evening the Lieutenant had been obliged to rush to Terre-Froide, where Catholics and Protestants had once more started fighting. Visibly not believing him, the priest contented himself with raising his eyes to heaven, affecting the air of a martyr, and the procession got under way again.

At the Oriani gate, which opened onto the highway, Father Le Bellec made the sign of the cross to ward Lucifer off his path. The crowd of the faithful, including the guards, quickly did the same, and they recited Pater Nosters, Ave Marias, and then the Credo, as the fog, gently sifting in from Montjoli, exhaled all around like incense a strong smell of pine and peppermint. And finally they repeated the opening hymn: "We want God, Virgin Mary . . ." They did the same thing at all the crossroads, places favorable above all others to evil spells, so it was nine o'clock when the procession reached the Fonds-Rouge section.

A triumphant smile curled the priest's lips and he became youthfully excited with the noble feeling that he was filling his double mission of priest and white man by leading into the paths of salvation this naïve flock of "fetishists," whose mentality, according to him, had not yet reached beyond the "prelogical" stage. He loved them well, however, in his way, and considered them all children of the Good Lord, who had created them more or less in His image.

Only he forgot or did not know that, despite one thousand five hundred years of Christianity, the prehistoric beliefs of his blue-eyed ancestors were still attached with deep and vigorous roots to the obstinate soil of old Armorica. Obsessed by Satan, as were the majority of his colleagues, he saw him everywhere in Haiti. And he was a long way from thinking like Joseph de Maistre that "superstition is an advanced work of religion that must not be destroyed." But he had kept almost intact the questionable faith and barbaric zeal of the Chouans.

Moreover, he always dated from "Boischandelle, Black Brittany" the letters he wrote his family and friends, and when he referred to his flock, it often happened that he called them "my Negroes" or sometimes "the natives," as if the country, in his eyes, was still "the colonies." Still, he meant no harm, and the fact is that color prejudice has so permeated the language of white people, bringing into it over the centuries, together with the confused notions of race, civilization, "primitiveness," a whole system of clichés and expressions unfavorable to the black man, that it would not be fair to accuse Father Le Bellec of racism. His attitude certainly sprang from a feeling of superiority; but could one justly reproach him for a secret vice whose existence he did not even suspect? It was, after all, but a cultural heritage and he had acquired it gradually, since his childhood, with the very language of his country.

So the Evil One had many disappointments in store for him. . . .

Estinval Civilhomme had left the procession behind; with hat in hand and surrounded by his children (with the exception of Eudovia Origène, who had been forbidden by her stern spouse, under threat of divorce, to take part in the ceremony), he was waiting for the priest at the entrance to his *habitation*.

The cottony whiteness of his hair and goatee suggested the idea that Papa Legba in person, renouncing the eminent position he held in the hierarchy of African gods, "was opening the gates" of the section to the enemies of vodou. But the sly old man genuflected and made the sign of the cross. Then, smiling as casually as a great planter welcoming guests to his domain, he led the procession toward his *houmfor,* before which were piled pell-mell all the objects sacred to the religion that he and his clients had just "rejected"—with the exception, of course, of the pearl necklace he said he'd received from the Spirits of the Water.

Since he intended to put plenty of vim into it, Father Le Bellec asked the congregation to kneel, made the sign of the cross, repeated by all the faithful, then recited the following invocation, with an inspired air and in a manly voice:

"Most glorious Prince of the heavenly host, St.

Michael the Archangel, protect us in the battle with the principalities and powers, against the chiefs of this world of darkness, against the evil spirits that fill the air. Come to the aid of men whom God has made in His image and likeness, and redeemed at so great a cost from the tyranny of the devil.

"It is you that the Holy Church worships as its guardian and protector; you to whom the Lord has entrusted the redeemed souls, so you may lead them to the joys of heaven. Beseech the God of peace to crush Satan beneath our feet, to take away all his power of keeping men captive henceforth, and of harming the Church. Offer our prayers to the Almighty, so that the mercy of the Lord may quickly descend upon us; seize with your own hands the ancient serpent, which is none other than the devil or Satan, to cast him into the depths in chains, so that he can no longer lead the nations astray.

"In the name of Jesus Christ, our Lord and God, with the intercession of the Immaculate Virgin Mary, Mother of God, St. Michael the Archangel, the Holy Apostles Peter and Paul and all the saints (and sustained by the sacred authority of our ministry), we make bold to repel the assaults and wiles of the devil."

Casting themselves down, face to the ground, the congregation proclaimed that it renounced Satan, his pomps and works. Father Le Bellec sprinkled the participants with holy water and gave them his benediction. Then he ordered the destruction of the *peristyle*— which was accomplished in the twinkling of an eye, with a frenzied zeal that was part enthusiasm and part anger. The wooden beams and the thatch of the *tonnelle*, as well as the chairs around the dance ring, were piled up in the courtyard, sprinkled with kerosene, and they made a huge fire, where they threw, one after the other, in a concert of imprecations which expressed the hatred of the converts, the conical drums, the banners, the ceremonial rattles decorated with snake vertebrae, the dishes used for offerings, the multicolored necklaces of the initiates, the terra-cotta *govis* containing the *loas* served by Estinval's clients—in short, all the accessories for the various vodou rites, including Catholic chromos, the crucifix, and other holy pictures which had been profaned for superstitious purposes.

The auto-da-fé was not ended when, at the request of the priest, the sacred trees around the *houmfor* were cut down while the crowd threw stones at them and screamed abuses against the *loas* who were supposed to live in them. These spirits, no doubt reduced to impotence by the intervention of St. Michael, offered no resistance to their eviction, but when the time came for the big black cross of Baron Samedi, the powerful guardian of cemeteries, a half-dozen patients in treatment at Estinval's, possessed by various *guédés,* burst into the courtyard. Gesticulating grotesquely and uttering the favorite obscenities of the spirits of the dead, they rushed in among the faithful, where they spread utter confusion, especially among the women, before whom they executed a belly dance. One of them, a big burly black fellow, stood squarely face to face with Father Le Bellec, arms akimbo, and said to him in a nasal voice: "It's me, Baron Samedi, talking to you. What do you think you're doing, knocking down my cross? It's made of wood, you can burn it. But I, who am a *loa* from Guinea, you won't burn me. You won't chase me away from this country, either."

On the order from Sergeant Fortuné, two soldiers seized him, but he struggled furiously, while another *guédé* burst out in a sardonic laugh.

"Hell!" cried another. "Just look at all those skirts no one has the nerve to lift up. Aren't you ashamed, sirs? Right now every last one of you should be in bed caressing his wife. One would think you are all impotent. If that's the case, we *guédés* are quite ready to replace you."

Thereupon he went and took, from what remained of the burned objects, a chair leg the flames had spared, put it between his legs like a phallus, and mimed the sexual act as he went toward the group of women. Horrified, they began screaming frantically. But Father Le Bellec, who had not lost his composure, had no trouble calming them down by reminding them that they were under the protection of the Lord.

Then going up to the patient possessed by Baron Samedi, still struggling in the grip of the soldiers, he held the crucifix to his forehead. The guardian of cemeteries, furious at this contact, howled like a madman.

"No, I won't go away. You can do what you want, I won't return to Guinea. Do you really believe I'm the devil?"

And the other *guédés* chorused his words.

"We won't go away," they said as they continued their lewd dance. "We won't leave. Besides, we have to sleep with all the women here. . . ."

Father Le Bellec had by no means anticipated such resistance, all the more surprising because he thought all of Estinval's clients had *rejected* after the Mass, including the ones who were presently possessed. But he was not surprised to the point of losing his poise. Taking the bull by the horns, he energetically recited this formula of exorcism, one of the most powerful in his arsenal:

"May God arise, and His enemies be banished and flee before Him those who hate Him.

"As smoke vanishes, may they disappear; as wax melts before fire, thus perish sinners before the face of God.

"Behold the cross of God, flee ye enemy powers.

"He has conquered, the lion of the tribe of Judah, the scion of David.

"May Thy mercy, oh Lord, be upon us, even as we have hoped in Thee.

"We exorcise you, unclean spirit, whoever you are, satanic power, invasion of the infernal spirit, legion, reunion, or satanic sect; in the name and by the virtue of Jesus Christ, our Lord, be rooted out and chased from God's Church, from the souls created in the image of God and redeemed by the precious blood of the divine Lamb. Henceforth you will no longer dare, perfidious serpent, deceive mankind, persecute the Church of God, neither shake nor winnow like wheat, the chosen of God. He commands you, God the Almighty, whom you in your great pride claim to resemble. He who wishes all men to be saved and that they attain knowledge of the truth. He, God the Father, commands you. He, God the Son, commands you. He, God the Holy Ghost, commands you. He, Christ, commands you, eternal Word of God made flesh, who, for the salvation of our race, lost by your jealousy, humbled Himself and rendered obedience until death, who built His Church on solid rock and promised that the gates of Hell would not prevail against her, wanting to remain with her all days until the consummation of the centuries. They command you, the sacred sign of the cross and the virtue of all the mysteries of the Christian faith. She commands you, the powerful Mother of God, the Virgin Mary, who, since the first moment of her Immaculate Conception, by her humility, crushed your proud head. It commands you, the faith of the holy apostles Peter and Paul and the other apostles. They command you, the blood of the martyrs and the pious intercession of all the saints.

"Now, cursed dragon and all the diabolic legion, we command you in the name of the living God, of the God who so loved the world that He gave His Only Begotten Son, that whosoever believes in Him shall not perish but may have life everlasting; desist from deceiving human creatures and from spreading the poison of eternal damnation, desist from harming the Church and impeding its freedom. Begone, Satan, inventor and master of all deceit, enemy of the salvation of mankind. Make way for Christ, in whom you have found none of your works; make way for the Church, united, holy, catholic and apostolic, which Christ Himself bought with His blood.

"Humble yourself beneath the powerful hand of God, tremble and flee at the invocation made by us, from the holy and terrible name of Jesus dreaded by Hell, to which the Virtues of the heavens, the Powers and Dominions are subject, whom the Cherubim and Seraphim praise in endless hymns, saying, Holy, Holy, Holy is the Lord, God of the heavenly host!"

This vigorous command of Father Le Bellec had no effect on the *guédés*, doubtless because he was using the wrong address—for in the belief of their servitors, the vodou spirits do not belong to hell but are, rather, auxiliaries of God. Seeing that the young priest was about to lose face, Estinval explained to him that the *mystères* of death do not understand French, and besides, the poor wretches he thought possessed of the devil were really incurable mental cases. The priest uttered a sigh of relief. Then he asked Sergeant Fortuné to order the guards to seize the insane patients, tie them up, and take them back to their padded cells—which was easily done with the help of the Soldiers of St. Michael, the *loas* having this in common with Satan, that it is not in their power to resist the police. Nevertheless, until the end, Baron Samedi and his acolytes kept on hurling obscenities and asserting that they would not leave the country.

Having gained control of the territory, Father Le Bellec, to crown the triumph of the Faith, had the *houmfor* set on fire. And since they had already sprinkled the principal beams of the sanctuary with kerosene, it flared up joyously into a smoke-laden apotheosis, attesting conclusively to the omnipotence of the Almighty.

Thereupon, the pious procession took shape again, and since it had a second mission of purifying the countryside around the town of Boischandelle, it started off in the direction of Bassin-Bleu, singing, "I am a Christian, that is my glory. . . ." But Estinval was taking no part in it. Pleading fatigue and his advanced age, the "old macaque," as his son-in-law called him, asked the priest to excuse him.

XII

The air was dry, the sky blue as a morning glory.

About a quarter of an hour before, the procession had left the highway and entered the byroad that crosses the pine wood of Kermeler, so that, with fewer people in each row, it had become longer. Until then, everything had proceeded in orderly fashion and the priest's endeavor seemed to promise success, when, as they were passing through the hamlet of Bussier, the Soldiers of St. Michael, who were bringing up the rear, bubbling over with aggressive joy, started up the martial hymn dear to the Lord of the heavenly host: "Let us march to battle, to glory . . ."

Father Le Bellec had advised them to observe the strictest restraint so as not to seem to provoke Josaphat's confraternity; but it was as though the aromatic smell of the mountain, warmed by the midday sun, had suddenly turned their heads.

Now the priest was quite far from these fanatics and could not go back to calm down their dangerous zeal. So, in spite of his apostolic courage, it was not without apprehension that he entered the section of Bassin-Bleu.

The members of the Trésor des Nagos society had gathered again. They were courageously awaiting the events that the Master of the House had announced to them. The drums were resounding with the same gusto as the night before, vigorously beating out the dance of the *canzos,* as the choir of the *bossales* sang stirring hymns in honor of Ogou Ferraille, who still possessed Josaphat's son. Dressed for the occasion in a red shirt and pants of blue cotton, a scarlet kerchief tied around his head, the warrior god was furiously pacing up and down the courtyard with his hands clasped behind his back. From time to time he would stop at the gate under the natural porch formed by two avocado trees and utter confused threats punctuated by vehement gestures. Then, before resuming his pacing up and down, by way of summary he would roar: "Let them come, my friends, let them come; I'll kill them all and drink their blood!"

However, as Boss Février advised him to do, Josaphat had disarmed his partisans of their machetes and had allowed them to keep only clubs. He had even taken away General Ogou's sword. Moreover, he had called on everyone to observe the greatest calm and not to fight unless the enemy came into the courtyard and attacked them. But he added, muttering between his teeth to show his determination: "We are ready. No *rejeté* can come and dictate to us, no matter how brave he is. If necessary, we'll fight like wild beasts, tigers, lions, elephants. And we'll see if the Soldiers of St. Michael are stronger than we are."

Soon the priest appeared on a rise at the head of the procession, holding the crucifix at the level of his face. Ogou Ferraille, without uttering a word, took a defiant stance at the gate, legs far apart and hands on his hips.

Meanwhile, sure of destroying "the forces of evil" in the long run, Father Le Bellec was advancing with dignity and measured tread, looking straight ahead. When finally he passed in front of Josaphat's *habitation,* he recited nonstop, in a firm and steady voice, the following invocation:

"God of the heavens, God of the earth, God of the Angels, God of the Archangels, God of the Patriarchs, God of the Prophets, God of the Apostles, God of the Martyrs, God of the Confessors, God of Virgins, God who has the power to give life after death, respite after toil, because there is no other God and there can be no other but you, the Creator of all things visible and invisible, whose reign will have no end; humbly we beseech your glorious Majesty to deign powerfully to deliver us and protect us from all power, snare, deceit, and malice of the infernal spirits. Through Jesus Christ our Lord. Amen."

"Amen!" said Ogou, in a mocking tone. *"Abobo!"*

The Children of Mary and the Ladies of the Third Order obeyed the wise instructions of the young priest and marched away without so much as a glance at Ogou or even at Josaphat's *houmfor.* They sang fervently but in their languid, insipid way, dragging out the last syllable of each line:

> I am a Christian, that is my glory,
> My hope and my strength;
> My song of love and victory:
> I am a Christian, I am a Christian.
> I am a Christian! At my baptism
> The holy water flowed over my brow;
> Grace, at that supreme moment,
> From my brow washed the stain. . . .

Josaphat's confraternity, finally reassured by the peaceful turn of events—for the enemy had not dared attack them directly or violently—gloated over it. Relying on appearances, they began to believe fully in their invincibility.

The drums throbbed with increasing intensity, the dance of the *canzos* became more vigorous and obsessive, and while the *hogantier's* iron bell strongly evoked the image of a forge in full activity and the *houngan* was hurling rum, gunpowder, and salt in Ogou's brazier to boost the flame and make it crackle loudly, the choir of the *bossales* extolled at the top of their lungs, with Dionysian fury, the triumph of the Master of the House:

Fer, Ogou Fer, Ogou Fer, Ogou Fer oh!
Fer, Ogou Fer, Ogou Fer, Ogou Fer oh!
Fer, Ogou Fer, Ogou Fer, Ogou Fer oh!
Dambala, I am firing the cannon, oh!
Fer, Ogou Fer, Ogou Fer, Ogou Fer oh!
Dambala, I am firing the cannon, oh!
Fer, Ogou Fer, Ogou Fer, Ogou Fer oh!
Dambala, I am firing the cannon, oh!

But the General, a "man of politics" who was supposed to know the future, did not join in the rejoicing of his faithful followers. He simply contented himself with a sneer as he looked at the pious procession of the *devotions* filing past, which he seemed to consider an amusing parade of strange beasts whose purpose was to benumb his vigilance.

"Hell!" he said at last, tired of hearing their none-too-soothing hymn. "My testicles are getting cold!"

Which meant, in his language of a tough old soldier,

that he was thirsty. They hurried, therefore, to bring him a full bottle of rum, but, contrary to his custom, he swallowed only half of it. Then, wiping his mouth politely with the back of his hand, he explained to the astonished faithful that on days of combat he drank moderately.

They had not finished praising his prudence when he noticed the turbulent troop of the Soldiers of St. Michael, which in turn was emerging from the pine wood and shouting with all their might:

> War to Satan, vile spirit,
> War to infamous sensuality,
> War to deceit, war to the world,
> To Jesus Christ, fidelity.
> Let's march to battle, to glory,
> Let's march in the footsteps of Jesus;
> We shall bring back victory,
> And the crown of the elect. . . .

The fun was over. Obviously, Ogou's prediction was about to come true. At least, that was the General's opinion. He went and found Josaphat, who was leading the wild dance of the *canzos* under the *peristyle,* all the while shaking the *asson* and the officiant's hand bell; and he brutally asked for his sword. The *houngan,* sticking to the advice of the town councilman Louis-Jean Février, refused to give it to him—to avert bloodshed, he said. A discussion arose during which the *mystère* and his priest got excited to the point of exasperation, while the music and dancing maintained a hallucinating atmosphere:

Fer, Ogou Fer, Ogou Fer, Ogou Fer oh . . .

The Soldiers of St. Michael finally reached Josaphat's property, and there they stopped on a command from their leader—a repentant *bush-priest* who always did as he pleased—and in a very aggressive way they began to recite the most offensive part of the new catechism which the Catholic Church was at that time teaching the peasants. The *bush-priest* asked the questions and the others answered in unison, as they did in Sunday school:

"Who is the principal slave of Satan?"

"The principal slave of Satan is the *houngan*."

"What are the names the *houngans* give Satan?"

"The names the *houngans* give Satan are *loas,* angels, saints, the dead, the *marassas*."

"For what reason do the *houngans* give the names of *loas,* angels, saints, and the dead to Satan?"

"*Houngans* give the names of *loas,* angels, saints, and the dead to Satan to deceive us more easily. . . ."

It was at this point that things took a bad turn. There is no way of knowing which of the two sides threw the first stone, but in the clash it sparked, the combatants on both sides showed the same zeal in stoning each other, as they ran for cover, behind a tree, a rock, or any other obstacle. There were heads broken and blood flowed, but this did not stop the music from getting more and more exalted:

Fer, Ogou Fer, Ogou Fer, Ogou Fer oh . . .

Finally, the guards, who were just ahead of the Soldiers of St. Michael, alerted by the noise of the clash, started back, and at the order of Sergeant Fortuné, fired a volley of shots over the head of the belligerents. In the confusion that ensued, a flyaway spark from Ogou's fire, whose logs had been kicked around by some of the fugitives, set fire to the thatch on the *peristyle*. And quickly, with the breeze just coming up, the flames reached the *houmfor*.

Just at that moment; the General was going into the sanctuary looking for his sword. They had tried in vain to dissuade him. He was still in there when the roof collapsed. So a great outcry of terror rose. But, to everyone's surprise, the *mystère* reappeared, miraculous and panting, brandishing his sword in the air. He stopped a moment to catch his breath. And since his clothes had caught fire and smoke was coming out of them, Josaphat poured over his head a pail of water he was holding in reserve for ritual libations.

Paying no attention to what was going on, Ogou Ferraille, who had not been burned at all, rushed up to the enemy, hurling insults. The Soldiers of St. Michael, scared to death, ran off in great disarray, taking Sergeant Fortuné and his men along as they fled.

Panic was quickly communicated to the rest of the procession, already upset by the gunfire and tumult of the clash. In the stampede that resulted, Father Le Bellec was so roughly jostled it was only by a hair's breadth that he missed losing his crucifix.

But the irascible Ogou was still not satisfied. He had been attacked in his sanctuary, and besides, it had burned down. And though he had routed the enemy, he felt his prestige had suffered, and so he resolved to take the war to the other camp. But Josaphat, having suffered material losses amounting to virtual ruin, thought that things had gone too far as it was. He declared bluntly that the Trésor des Nagos society would not go along with the General on that adventure.

XIII

In the afternoon, a strong wind from the sea, driving immense black clouds, savagely passed over the region. A torrential rain came in its wake and fell without letup until nightfall, leaving behind a thick fog. It still cloaked, like a wet, cold blanket, the hillock where the town of Boischandelle rose in tiers, when, at the stroke of midnight, the church bells, for no reason, started sounding the alarm.

Father Le Bellec, who was sleeping like a log, regaining his strength after the labors and agitation of the day, woke with a start and, as he later related to the archsee, "with a leap" got out of bed, seized his revolver "loaded to the hilt," and went downstairs in his nightclothes.

But let's hear the young priest himself:

"I went out under the balcony of the rectory. 'Who's there?' No answer; the bells are still ringing. 'What are you doing there?' No answer. I fire my gun in the air. That doesn't seem to faze the rash fellow hanging on my bells. Then I went and finished dressing and started out, gun in hand, yelling for help. My man had left the bells but, armed with a crowbar, had lifted the church door and gone inside. The neighbors, alarmed by the firing of my gun followed by my stirring call for help, gathered to lend their support. Two big strapping fellows followed me inside the church, where I found the self-appointed bell-ringer sitting in my celebrant's armchair. My companions had armed themselves with enormous hardwood clubs, as a precautionary measure. The rascal made no response to our demand that he clear out, so he got an appropriate beating. But the more blows he got, the more he persisted in keeping his seat. . . ."

He was still there when Fortuné arrived, escorted by three guards. The Sergeant was quite excited, wondering what in the world could be going on at such an hour in the holy place. By the diffused glow of the perpetual light, he finally made out the intruder, whose swollen face was streaming with blood, and quickly recognized him, thanks to his getup and sickly look, as the son of Josaphat. Struck with horror and pity, he put a quick stop to the beating, which he found incongruous in a church, pushed Father Le Bellec's "strapping fellows" away from their victim, and tried to negotiate with Ogou, who, since he possessed Dieudonné, was wholly responsible, in his opinion, for the violation of the sanctuary.

"Ferraille, what are you doing here?" he asked calmly, affecting a stern expression. "Do you take this church for a *houmfor?*"

"You dare ask me what I'm doing here!" replied the *mystère* arrogantly. "It's true the church is not a *houmfor,* but isn't it the house where Papa the Good Lord receives his children when they have something to tell or ask Him? And am I not His child like all the other saints?"

"You tell me you're a child of the Good Lord. Since I

know nothing about that, I won't contradict you. But this is no hour to come into the church. You are breaking the law, and I have to arrest you."

"Arrest me, General Ogou Ferraille! You aren't crazy, no? A little fish like you! If it was Lieutenant Bellami, I wouldn't object, no. But you're just a sergeant!"

"Lieutenant is at Terre-Froide. In his absence, I'm in charge here. So you have to obey me."

"Obey you, a worthless little louse! Have you lost your head completely?"

"As you can see, Ferraille, it's solidly in place on my two shoulders. But that's not the question. You entered this church in the dead of night, after forcing the door. The law obliges me to arrest you."

"If you think you can do it, you idiot, you just try it and see."

Scowling at this insulting challenge, Sergeant Fortuné, whose patience was at an end, ordered his guards to take hold of Ogou Ferraille. What happened then would be hard to believe even by the most gullible, if the indignant testimony of Father Le Bellec were not available to corroborate it. Despite the ridiculously light weight of Dieudonné, the guards did not succeed in moving him off the armchair, for, said the priest, "Satan had caused the possessed one to become as heavy as a truckload of rocks."

Couldn't one wonder, however, if this abnormal weight were not an illusion created by the superstitions of those who experienced it? But the priest of Boischandelle was incapable of posing such a question, which would have exonerated Lucifer, especially since the priest shared the belief of the Reverend Father Ravignan that the greatest ruse of the devil has been "to make himself denied."

"I was sure you would not succeed in getting hold of this rascal," he said coldly to the Sergeant. "He is possessed of the devil, and only a minister of God can manage it. Let me exorcise him, so you will finally be able to arrest him."

Sergeant Fortuné, convinced of his own powerlessness, but having little faith in the efficacy of exorcism, readily accepted and gave a free hand to the priest, who went into the sacristy to get a crucifix, holy water, and an aspergillum. But when the priest approached the possessed boy, the latter "leapt like a wild animal" and bit him cruelly on the shoulder, "with his sharp and firmly rooted canines piercing through" the cassock and shirt of the young cleric.

The guards had not recovered from their surprise when Ogou went and sat down again licking his lips, while his victim, horrified, bolted from the holy place to go and dress his wound. Sergeant Fortuné, not knowing what to do, ordered his men to keep an eye on the General while he went to get the Justice of the Peace, followed by Father Le Bellec's neighbors and the curious onlookers who had gathered in front of the church during the incident.

Although Septimus Morency was supposed to be a light sleeper, Fortuné knocked on his door a long while without getting any answer. He even threw some stones up to the roof of the house and yelled as loud as he could: "Justice Morency! Justice Morency! It's Sergeant Fortuné."

Discouraged, he was on the point of leaving when he heard coming from upstairs the noise of a chair knocked over, then a body falling to the floor, and he thought he made out the sound of a woman's quickly stifled moans.

114

Whereupon someone hurriedly went down the stairs, as if in a panic, and turned the key in the lock. And as the Sergeant turned on his flashlight, the door opened with a great to-do.

"By the thundering Jupiter, what do you want of me at this tardy hour of the sacred repose of night?"

The Justice of the Peace, in underpants and a flannel undershirt, flashed at Fortuné a glance burning with Olympian wrath. The latter stammered out an excuse and related as best he could what had happened in the church.

"Mr. Justice," he said finally, "I came to get you so you could go and record the incident and draw up your report. And who knows? Since you are an authority, maybe Ferraille will obey an order from you and finally submit to being arrested."

"If I'm to judge by what I see," said Septimus, raising his eyes to the heavens, "our poor city of Boischandelle is irreparably co-rrupted! All the licentious deities of the African pantheon have banded together to disturb the refreshing sleep of the champions of order and Greco-Roman spirituality. What can I do about it? I shall therefore go, Sergeant Fortuné, to draw up a report in the divine sanctuary profaned by the flagrant Satanism of vodouistic mysticism and proceed to arrest the lawbreaker. In the meantime, dear friend, please allow me to go and finish dressing in the decent attire of a respectable man."

As the Justice of the Peace was going up the stairs to the second floor, there was a rustling of leaves in the avocado tree that brushed against the balcony of the house, and a woman—perched, it seemed, at the same spot—plaintively sang:

> Erzilie was married three times,
> She had no luck!
> Erzilie was *placée* three times,
> She had no luck!
> Erzilie tried the prostitute's life three times,
> She had no luck!

It was one of the favorite hymns of Erzilie Fréda Dahomey, the goddess of love and the acknowledged mistress of Ogou, and the people gathered in front of Septimus Morency's door thought they recognized the cooing inflections of La Paloma's voice. They were not mistaken. As the fog lifted, the moon appeared on the horizon and they had no trouble identifying the singer, who, with only a nightgown on, her hair disheveled, was perched on top of the tree, pulling off the leaves in handfuls and dropping them with affected youthful grace.

At that very moment, Bellami was getting home from Terre-Froide. He wondered why there was a crowd, but Fortuné did not have time to tell him about the events of that night. La Paloma started singing again:

> Erzilie was married three times . . .

The Lieutenant was astonished and his shame was extreme. To prevent anyone's saying that Dulce María served the *mystères* (or something even more humiliating), he explained to the Sergeant that she was subject to somnambulism. Then, paying no attention to the muted laughter of the skeptics, he went into his house and got a bedspread, had four strong men hold it taut under the avocado tree, nimbly climbed up to the top of the tree like a fireman, and picked up his wife. She offered no resistance and continued to sing as he helped her down from branch to branch.

Septimus Morency had dressed in the interim, and as soon as La Paloma was taken back under the marital roof and put to bed, he went to the church with the Lieutenant and his Sergeant, as a muffled, annoying uproar rose from the crowd of the curious following them.

This time, Ogou Ferraille was in a more accommodating humor. To Bellami's courteous remonstrances, he replied that he willingly accepted being arrested by an officer.

"But," he said, "those little mosquitoes (that is, the little priest, the Sergeant, and your guards) have no right to give me orders or to touch me. They are lucky I didn't reduce them to dust. If it wasn't for the respect I owe to Papa the Good Lord . . ."

He shook his head, gnashed his teeth, and finally said: "Lieutenant, take me to your office. There we can talk quietly, as man to man."

At the Garde d'Haiti station, Ogou aired his grievances at great length. He told how the *houmfor* of Josaphat Joseph had been attacked by the Soldiers of St. Michael, described the clash that followed, the burning of the temple, where he still was when the roof collapsed, and he bragged for having, all by himself, routed the attackers. But, he pointed out, the losses sustained by his priest were considerable, without counting that his own prestige had suffered from it. So it was by way of reprisal that he had broken into the church, after sounding the alarm.

"I understand very well that you can be angry," said the Lieutenant. "But I cannot approve of the way you have chosen to take revenge, especially since Josaphat could bring legal action and justice would be rendered him."

"Yeah!" said Ogou, sarcastically. "Justice would be rendered him! Then tell me what Sergeant Fortuné and his squad were doing among the Soldiers of St. Michael and why they fired on the *houmfor?*"

"No, General, they couldn't have done that. It was surely shots in the air that they fired to put an end to the disturbance."

"Yeah! And that's why they didn't have a clear conscience and fled with the little priest's bandits when, with sword in hand, I took the offensive?"

"I don't know," said Bellami, who was getting edgy. "Sergeant Fortuné hasn't made his report yet. Besides, that's not the point. You committed a sacrilege by breaking into the church tonight after you forced the door open. And on top of that, you bit Father Le Bellec on the shoulder. . . ."

"He had just had my head broken by his partisans," retorted Ogou.

"Excuse me, General," said the Lieutenant, curtly. "I'll have to consider your case with Justice Sèpe to determine what decision to take regarding you."

In order to save himself from the tirades of the god of war, he steered the Justice of the Peace into another room and said to him in a low voice, as though confiding a state secret: "Sèpe, old fellow, this affair is full of shit, yes!"

"Irritating, dear friend," corrected Septimus, shocked but conciliatory. "Let's say rather that it is irritating."

The Officer didn't see any difference, as far as he was concerned. Therefore, after quick reflection, he went straight to the problem that was bothering him: to determine who was to be charged, Dieudonné Joseph or the General. Since the law does not recognize the gods, the simplest solution was to accuse the young man, but this seemed unjust to him because, in fact, Ogou was the real culprit and his *horse* had no awareness of what had happened.

"That is, however, my noble Centurion, the stern task that we must dauntlessly accomplish," declared Septimus Morency, pompously. "To plead his innocence, you offer the controversial fact that Dieudonné was possessed, but that excuse does not exonerate him any more from penitentiary expiation and *pretium doloris* than if he had been under the intoxicating influence of Bacchus. Consequently, it certainly is he who should be indicted. There is no need for us to fracture our occipital bone with the casuistical quibbles of the vodou practitioners, which have, in law and in fact, neither rhyme nor reason. I visualize certainly that the affair is as thorny as a desert forest of cactaceae, and I confess that as far as my modest juridical self is concerned, I would gladly rinse my digital phalanges in the expeditious manner of Pontius Pilatus, for Josaphat Joseph is blindly devoted to the town councilman Louis-Jean Février, who, in turn, fully enjoys the nepotistic protectorate of the Minister of the Interior. Moreover, we can vaticinate that the Breton clan, making use of the combustible altitude of the pulpit and the flashing columns of their printed mouthpiece, will stir up a commotion that will surpass purgatory or even hell in caloric power. And that is why, at this early hour of the matutinal darkness, I would advise you, in all wisdom, to return to the fragrant bed of your legal cohabitant and leave our General in the safe custody of preventive incarceration, while we wait for the dazzling resurrection of the diurnal star. Then, dear friend, we shall dispatch him under good escort to Port-au-Prince, where they will peremptorily mete out to his *horse* an appropriate punishment. As for me, I am going this instant to make my report—which the unpropitious luminary in the church did not permit me to draw up on the spot."

After a moment of pathetic silence, he added: "I have already drawn up an official report on the incendiary clash at Bassin-Bleu, covering the sortie *extra muros* of the Reverend Father Le Bellec, that edifying periplus, praiseworthy in theory but deplorable in practice, which he thoughtlessly undertook, violating the Sunday peace of the sector of Boischandelle instead of teaching the catechism under the Edenic boughs of the lofty eucalyptus fast by the rectory entrance."

The Justice of the Peace took leave of Lieutenant Bellami, and Ogou Ferraille was, after all, booked under the name of Dieudonné Joseph.

XIV

As he was being transferred to Port-au-Prince, Ogou Ferraille behaved rather well, except that he swore once in a while and complained some of having cold testicles. He behaved the same in prison. But in the examining magistrate's office he was very annoyed by the judge's attitude, for the latter pretended not to know him and addressed him only as Dieudonné Joseph. If he had done his utmost to be arrested, it was so he could take to court his defense of the *loas* and to attack the brutal conduct of the Catholic clergy toward the followers of vodou. Realizing that they would use all possible means to prevent him from doing it, he lost his patience and abandoned his *horse* after haughtily announcing that he was going to the battlefields of the world war, where, he claimed, he had plenty to do.

Dieudonné fell to the floor as though he had been struck by lightning, and sank into a coma. Rushed to the hospital, he died a few days later, apparently—if we can believe the doctors—from the effects of the terrible beating that the priest's "strapping fellows" had given him in the church of Boischandelle.

Meantime, the Port-au-Prince papers had made a lot of noise about the clash at Bassin-Bleu and the burning of Josaphat's *houmfor,* casting all the blame on the Reverend Father Le Bellec, while *Le Faisceau,* the official paper of the archdiocese, had settled for publishing, *in extenso,* the young priest's report. But after Dieudonné's opportune death, which still caused quite a stir, the two sides toned down their quarrel by tacit agreement, and the affair fizzled out, at least in the capital, for, in Boischandelle, passions were at their height and people continued discussing the events that had so recently troubled the tranquillity of the commune.

It also happened, by a singular coincidence, that at the precise moment the General's *mount* was dying—it was a Sunday after High Mass—Father Le Bellec had a pall hung in the chancel between four chandeliers, and with the faithful had sung a Miserere to beg forgiveness of God for the public outrage of which He had been the object, then a Libera for the poor souls in Purgatory. This was all it took for him to be accused of magic and considered responsible for the death of the young man. His partisans, beginning with Estinval, cast the blame in vain on Ogou Ferraille, who, according to them, was punishing Josaphat for not supporting him in the profanation of the church. Appearances were against the priest. And things got worse when he refused to give Dieudonné a church burial, because, he said, the deceased had committed a sacrilege and given up his soul without being absolved of a most grievous mortal sin.

The picturesque adventure of Madame Bellami, which under different circumstances would have been the subject of endless commentary, scarcely occupied people's minds and was already almost forgotten. But

Boss Louis-Jean Février, the town councilman, eager to ruin the Justice of the Peace because of his closeness with the Mayor, never missed an opportunity to keep it alive. For this mean purpose, any pretext served him well, and sometimes he did not even bother to have one. Thus, on the day the Boar of the Mountain brought back from Port-au-Prince Dieudonné's body, he noticed Rénélus Altidor filling up at the market gas station, and he yelled out: "Hullo, Rénélus! Hullo, old fellow!"

"Beg pardon, boss?"

"When you're through, come by for a little chat. I haven't seen you for over two weeks!"

Rénélus made a face, for he had a good idea of what was coming up. But could he avoid it? Jealous as he was of La Paloma, he felt cruelly offended by the episode of the avocado tree. Everyone in Boischandelle knew she was his mistress. Ever since he discovered her completely naked in the company of Alcius, they didn't miss a chance to laugh in his face. A practical joker from around there had even made up a song about it and the urchins hummed it when he went by. And now that gossip of a Boss Février was going to have some fun by turning the sword in the wound!

In fact, they had hardly exchanged the standard greeting when the town councilman asked him point-blank: "Between us, old fellow, do you think when they went to get the Justice of the Peace for the unfortunate incident at the church that Madame Bellami was really possessed by Mistress Erzilie?"

"Han!" said Rénélus, scratching the back of his head. "How would I know? Lieutenant says his wife is a *somambulist*, that she has the habit of walking in her sleep."

"Yeah, old fellow, yeah!" said Boss Février with the

trace of a smile. "That's what poor Charles-Oscar says to avoid scandal and to whitewash his lawful wife. But I've always known—at least, that's what I've heard since I was a boy—that somnambulists go about their nocturnal exploits with their eyes closed and without talking at all. Now, according to the irrefutable testimony of all those present, La Paloma's eyes were wide open and she was melodiously singing one of the favorite airs of Erzilie Fréda Dahomey."

"In that case, boss," said Rénélus Altidor, his voice flat from repressed anger, "I'd be inclined to think that Mistress really did *mount* Madame Bellami."

"So would I, old fellow, so would I; that would be my inclination, all the more so because—and it's a delicate point I call to your closest attention, for you know as I do the free and easy ways of the libidinous goddess of love—all the witnesses report that before he opened the door, with very few clothes on, the Justice of the Peace had been having a rather lively discussion with a woman whose voice and La Paloma's were as much alike as two drops of water. Besides, Septimus had scarcely conferred with the Sergeant and gone back upstairs to dress properly when La Paloma in her nightgown was singing in the tree next to the balcony of his house. Possessed or not, no one in this town doubts that she was enjoying herself voluptuously with her neighbor when Sergeant Fortuné came knocking at the door, and that, intent on not interrupting her pleasure, she tried to hold back the dear man in the copulative embrace. Whence the discussion they heard . . ."

He took a deep breath, pretended to be rapt in thought, shook his head and continued: "It's possible, nevertheless, that La Paloma gave herself to Septimus in full lucidity, to thank him for having intervened at the crucial moment when you had taken her by the throat and were about to strangle her. Wouldn't you agree, old fellow?"

And as the driver of the Boar of the Mountain, in a paroxysm of rage, was on the point of denying he had been about to assassinate his mistress, Boss Février added casually: "Oh, you know, Septimus reported the matter to the Origènes, who, for their part, didn't feel they should make a secret of it, since you were accusing Alcius of having attempted rape on the person of Madame Bellami."

"Justice Morency is a saint," declared Rénélus Altidor, to change the subject. "In the five years he's been here, you've never heard that he was mixed up with a woman."

"That's a fact I won't deny, old fellow. But Septimus is not a saint, he's a hypocrite. At the end of every month, you drive him to Port-au-Prince, where he spends three or four days, and you know as well as I do that while he's there he goes to the Frontier every evening so he can give full satisfaction to a natural urge that torments men as well as animals."

Just then they caught sight of Josaphat Joseph crossing the marketplace and running in their direction. Shaken by Father Le Bellec's refusal, he was coming to tell Boss Février about it, in the foolish hope that the latter would intercede on his behalf, and thanks to the prestige of his position, he might prevail on the young priest to change his decision. Rénélus felt greatly relieved when he saw the *houngan* coming. He leaned familiarly toward the town councilman and said to him in a low voice: "It isn't true, no, that I was going to choke Dulce María. We were only having a friendly little quarrel. Justice Morency couldn't have said anything else. But the Origènes, to clear Alcius, made more of it than he told them."

Then, touching the brim of his big black hat, he took his leave. Josaphat waited until the bus driver reached the gas station to say to his *compère* without preamble: "Yet, my son was baptized!"

Thereupon he burst into sobs. Although Boss Février was a hardened egotist indifferent to everything not directly concerned with his political career, he could not help but be moved. He laid his hand affectionately on the *houngan*'s shoulder and tried to comfort him.

"I see what the trouble is," he said. "The little priest refused to give my godson a church burial?"

"That's exactly it," confirmed Josaphat in a broken voice, sniffling. "He told me all he could do was to recite the last prayer for the deceased Dieudonné in front of the church. But I can't bury my son like a dog. Papa the Good Lord would not be willing to receive him."

"There's a way to get around it, my good man. You know that the Lord in His infinite goodness makes no distinction between Christians, whether Catholic or Protestant. And it happens, by chance, that Pastor Bienaimé, before being converted to Pentecostalism, was a *houngan* like you. He won't refuse, I'm sure, to offer the service for the dead over the mortal remains of your son."

"And he won't ask me to *reject* before the burial?"

"He won't ask you that, my good man. Afterwards, he might. Right now, the problem is not you but my late godson. Besides, doesn't your daughter Hortense go to his church already?"

"Not any more, Mr. Councilman. I stopped her going because that's where she met that worthless Alcius, the little *resté-avec* of the Origènes. They intended to marry, but I'd rather die than give my daughter to a servant. The trouble is that the pastor seemed to encourage them in their plan."

"Never mind that; Bienaimé is a friend of mine. I'll go see him in a minute and I'll give you his answer right away after our conversation. In the meantime, go back home in all confidence, and take care of the preparations for the burial."

Actually, the town councilman immediately obtained the consent of the pastor, who shared his opinion that a Christian is always a Christian, whatever his persuasion.

He was a giant with stooped shoulders, always dressed in black, who never left the house without a Bible tucked under his arm. When he was about thirty years old and already a highly reputed *houngan,* he contracted tuberculosis as the consequence of a chill he caught at the falls at Saut d'Eau, where he had bathed while possessed by Sim'bi. His family *loas,* evoked in succession, were not able to effect a cure, so he gave up serving them and was converted to Protestantism. And since he was of robust constitution, a doctor whom he had had the good sense to consult succeeded in putting him back on his feet. Then, after some theological studies in Port-au-Prince as well as in the United States, he became, thanks to his extensive knowledge of vodou, one of the most effective adversaries of the popular beliefs of the country.

Concerning "supernatural illnesses," it seems he accomplished cures that looked like miracles, just by invoking the Holy Ghost. But what helped him most of all in his ministry was that up to a certain point, by its dances and crises of possession, his religion was akin to the peasants'.

The day after the town councilman's visit, the pastor,

accompanied by certain members of his church, called on Josaphat Joseph to start the funeral. The whole family, as well as the members of the Trésor des Nagos society, were gathered in the churchyard while Dieu-donné's body was on view under the arbor that sheltered the door of the house. The Pentecostalists went and crouched down around the coffin, and Bienaimé opened the prayer book *Songs of Hope* to the chapter of "Appeals" and intoned the following hymn:

> Jesus is calling you, oh! come and see
> Your Savior nailed to the Cross;
> For you, the King of heaven
> Came to shed His precious blood.

And, rhythmically clapping their hands, his acolytes began to chorus in unison:

> Jesus saves, Jesus saves,
> Jesus saves today
> All who come
> All who come
> All who come to Him. . . .

Suddenly, a hallucinated man started running and shouting like a madman: "The corpse moved! The corpse moved! The corpse moved. . . ."

There was a scuffle in the courtyard. Ogou Ferraille, having liberated the soul of the deceased, had just taken possession of Brutus, the elder son of Josaphat, and was roughly mounting and breaking in his new *horse*.

"Begone, Satan!" said the pastor in a powerful voice, while the members of his church, possessed of the Holy Ghost, were moaning and writhing with convulsions.

Ogou was growling and leaping around chaotically, sowing panic all around him. The only one who kept his wits about him in this hysterical atmosphere was Josaphat. He seized the General around the waist and, thanks to the power that *houngans* can exert over the *loas*, carried him, kicking, inside the house; but he had a hard time keeping him there. Foaming with rage, the spirit of war and fire was trying to shake loose from his grip.

"I certainly have the right to attend my *horse*'s funeral, hell!" he howled. "I came for it from far away."

"We wouldn't see any harm in it if you behaved properly," said Josaphat sternly. "But you were acting like a little boy riding a broomstick. If you think that's the way to attend a funeral . . ."

He calmed him down finally by offering him a bottle of rum to warm up his gonads and promised to organize a beautiful ceremony in his honor as soon as he rebuilt his *houmfor*. With this assurance, the General agreed to leave. And Pastor Bienaimé was able to perform Dieudonné's funeral in peace.

We must also say that Lieutenant Bellami, with a squad of guards, had been on hand to protect the cortège as well as the Pentecostalist church, for there were rumors that the Soldiers of St. Michael, egged on by Estinval, were plotting a new attack.

XV

Having learned that Macdonald Origène was in bed with a bad cold, Septimus Morency went to see him. His visit also had another motive. He had just received news from Port-au-Prince that he considered disturbing, and he was impatient to tell his friend about it.

The day before, the first Friday of the month, while the Low Mass of four o'clock was being celebrated, agents of the secret police fired shots in three churches of the capital, throwing the attendants into such a panic that some of them, especially women, old men, and children, were knocked down and trampled as people fled.

Honest Septimus was fuming with indignation.

"Were I not congenitally impecunious," he said, ending his report, "I would aristocratically hurl at the hirsute head of the government a sharply motivated missive of resignation."

Then, lowering his eyes, he made a vague gesture of discouragement and added pitifully: "But, alas! since I have to eat just like everyone else . . ."

Although he was coifed in his wife's purple polka-dot

kerchief, his neck softly swathed in an old flannel under-shirt, and he smelled strongly of oil of turpentine and mentholated vaseline, the Mayor of Boischandelle main-tained his solemn and imposing mask.

"Sèpe, my dear fellow, what are you telling me?" he asked, outraged. "It seems to me . . . uh . . . uh . . . there is something awfully wrong with you. Only yesterday you were patriotically professing an absolute respect for our august mentor, the President of the Republic . . . weren't you? Isn't that so? . . . 'The Chief,' you were saying with a sincere devotion which seemed indefectible . . . and now, on the strength of a few unverified rumors, you are on the point, like a new St. Peter . . . uh . . . uh . . . to deny the savior of our beloved country, which the shameless Pétainist Breton clergy are Machiavellistically trying to plunge into the chaos . . . are they not? . . . of a religious war."

"Gently, dear friend, gently!" said the Justice of the Peace sadly. "The legitimate virulence of my indignant speech certainly exceeded the result of my cervical activ-ity. In stipulating 'the hirsute head of the government' it was not my intent to aim, either close up or from a distance, at the venerated and prestigious head of the spiritualist son of the sublime mother of the Gracchi. That was just a calamitous slip. . . . I was aiming only at the dropsical head, with a deficient hair system, of the ambivalent minister who titularly holds the two offices, often twin departments, of Justice and Interior. . . . However, Mayor Origène, the horrific occurrences I've faithfully reported to you are by no means apocryphal. Prior to this friendly interview, the Centurion Bellami and I, your humble servant, made a few inquiring telephone calls to some of our ultra-veridical associates, and these facts, which you suspiciously qualify as rumors, were established by the strictest tangibility. I am only awaiting the wrathful reaction of the infallible patriarch of the Haitian nation, whom I deem foreign to these incongruous and immoral activities, deserving of the severest and most dishonorable legal punishment. Just visualize, dear friend: machine-gunning in holy places!"

Macdonald Origène felt caught up in Septimus Morency's indignation. Still, he judged it wise not to show his feeling immediately, since it was not his way to commit himself lightly. He made it a rule to be loyal to any government that did not threaten his being Mayor of Boischandelle, which he had, so to speak, inherited from his father, the late Sixtequint, nicknamed "Iron Pants." But there were higher principles dictated by conscience which he deemed it dishonest to compromise. And, having some means, by the grace of God, he was not, like the Justice of the Peace, subject to the plebeian servitude of owing his bread to the sweet will of the Chief of State . . . you see. . . . But he did have political ambitions, which was a hunger like any other, not any less exacting, and it made him completely vulnerable to the temptations of opportunism.

"After due consideration, Justice Sèpe," he finally said, "I think you are perfectly right . . . uh . . . uh . . . don't you see? . . . We should, in all wisdom, wait for the Chief's reaction. For my part, I don't for a minute doubt that he will condemn the perpetrators of these blasphemous disorders and that he will take . . . don't you see? . . . the drastic measures necessary."

He coughed and blew his nose with dignity. Then, anxious to drop a subject he considered delicate, to say the least, he said maliciously but in his most innocuous way to the Justice of the Peace: "Still, I heard that Bellami has been giving you the cold shoulder since the memorable night . . . uh . . . uh . . . you remember . . . when he found his wife perched, like a harebrained chicken, on your feeder tree."

"But why should he, dear friend?" asked Septimus, with raised eyebrows, although he knew perfectly well what the Mayor was driving at. "Why should he erect the hostile and rough wall of enmity between us? Didn't he, on his own, state *urbi et orbi* that his legal cohabitant was frequently prey to erratic crises of noctambulism?"

"Somnambulism," corrected Macdonald Origène.

"It's one and the same, dear friend, one and the same . . . or rather, to express myself more specifically, it's six of one and half a dozen of the other," protested the Justice of the Peace, justly annoyed.

And quickly seizing the opportunity, he tried to change the direction of the conversation. "If you were, as I am, an avid lexicologist, if you didn't just leaf through the *Petit Larousse Illustré*—'that manual of bourgeois thought,' as it is sharply defined by a young author friend of mine, who is unfortunately tainted with Muskovite Judeo-Marxism—if, now and then, you ventured a hunting safari into the game-filled jungle of the *Littré*, if you were, as much as I, steeped in semantic word-slides, if, I say . . . if . . ."

"Excuse me, gentlemen," said Madame Origène softly, as she brought in a steaming egg punch to her austere husband.

Septimus Morency was grateful to her for the interruption.

"Bovine Eudovia!" he said courteously.

She smiled with pleasure, and the Justice of the

Peace—admiring her gleaming white teeth set off by purple gums and satiny black skin, fresh as a cainito picked at dawn after the rain—thought she was the most beautiful woman in the world; but his contemplation—purely aesthetic, to tell the truth—was of short duration.

"Justice Sèpe," asked Eudovia, "wouldn't you like a little glass of rum to accompany Mac?"

"I can't refuse, dear friend," he said, rising and in a hurry to leave. "But at the praetorium in Boischandelle there's some urgent business I should not leave too long in abeyance."

Madame Origène couldn't in the least make out the Justice of the Peace's fine speech, but she guessed by his manner that he wanted to leave. She had heard the Mayor's question concerning his relations with Lieutenant Bellami. And like her husband, she was dying to know if the upright Septimus had slept with La Paloma, as all Boischandelle accused him of doing.

"Oh-ohhh!" she said with feigned surprise. "Why are you in such a hurry, Mr. Justice? You just came and you want to leave already, while your friend Mac is bored to death in bed. Besides, he has to talk to you about a serious matter that concerns you. When you came, I was just going to send my godchild Alcius to ask you to come by and see us."

"Really?" asked Septimus, embarrassed, strongly feeling he wouldn't be let off so easily.

But Eudovia was already on her way out of the bedroom.

"Please have a chair, dear friend," said the Mayor. "Madame Origène is offering you a glass of rum . . . uh . . . uh . . . isn't she? . . . If you don't accept, she could be deeply offended . . . you see . . . and needlessly complicate our friendly relations. You know women!"

"Very little, dear friend, very little!" said the Justice of the Peace, imprudently.

"But that's not what people say."

"And what, great God, can they say about the scrupulous praetor of the city of Boischandelle, whose Spartan virtue and Stylite continence are known a thousand leagues round?"

"They say . . . uh . . . uh . . . you see . . ."

"That La Paloma was doing a *belle* with you when Sergeant Fortuné knocked at your door the night of the sacrilege," said Madame Origène irreverently as she brought in the rum and bluntly finished her worthy husband's reply.

"A . . . a what, dear friend?"

"A *belle,* Justice Sèpe, a *belle!*"

"A *belle* . . . what do you mean by that?"

"That she was doing the thing gratis with you. . . . Why are you putting on the look of a little Jesus in the guise of a crab? Aren't you an old habitué of the Frontier?"

"Madame Origène," said the Mayor in a conciliatory tone, "it's a question of . . . you see . . . a delicate question . . . thorny even, should I say . . . and Justice Sèpe couldn't express himself relevantly . . . you see, don't you see? . . . without offending the virginal modesty of your devout ears . . . uh . . . uh . . . Let the two of us have a private chat, dearest, I beg of you."

Madame Origène scornfully shrugged her shoulders and withdrew without a word, her head held high—a veritable basalt goddess—but resolutely decided to eavesdrop, so she could hear the "relevant" confession of the Justice of the Peace.

"Justice Sèpe," said the Mayor solemnly, "you are not unaware that the individual named Louis-Jean Février . . . the satanic annotator of the no less diabolic Machiavelli . . . uh . . . uh . . . you see . . . anxious to replace me as President of the Town Council of Boischandelle, and knowing about our cordial friendship . . . for the last five years . . . don't you see? . . . is trying every possible way to get at me through you?"

"Actually, dear friend, I am not unaware of the wild megalomaniac ambitions of that unscrupulous individual, speculator in export goods. But, please enlighten me, what part do I have in his infernal and underhanded maneuvers?"

"He considers you, I think, the chink in my armor . . . don't you see? . . . although the thing, only a feeling, isn't easy to explain. . . . The fact is, nevertheless, that he publicly holds it against you that you did not have Alcius arrested for attempted rape . . . uh . . . uh . . . on the false accusation, laden with treachery, of Rénélus Altidor, which he pretends to consider the truth . . . you see . . . for this arrest would have put us, Madame Origène and me . . . so to speak . . . in a fine mess!"

"How then, merciful heavens, how could I, Septimus Morency, shamelessly get involved in criminal collusion with this automobilistic impostor, jealous cuckolder of a poor Centurion suffering from matrimonial blindness?"

"Whatever it is . . . uh . . . uh . . . you see . . . the town councilman Louis-Jean Février insinuates to anyone willing to listen that by not taking action against Madame Origène's godchild, you were in cahoots with the Mayor of Boischandelle. . . . And now, after the mysterious affair of the avocado tree . . . uh . . .

uh . . . he accuses you of having adulterous intimacy with Madame Bellami . . . and even of sexual depravities perpetrated openly and regularly in the brothels of the Frontier . . . uh . . . uh . . . don't you see? . . . Now, you are certainly aware that the Chief . . . although public rumor . . . very confused, of course, very hush-hush . . . based on scanty evidence, absolutely unverifiable . . . would have it that he is violently fond of the fair sex . . . uh . . . uh . . . you are not unaware, I say, that our revered mentor, as far as public employees are concerned . . . you see . . . is of the strictest severity on the subject of morality."

"Actually, as you have just expressed the indulgent hypothesis, I am not unaware that a homicidal sword . . . nay, bloodthirsty, one might say . . . is hanging over our innocent heads, Afro-Latin Damocles that we are!"

"Therefore, Justice Sèpe, you fully realize that as far as we are concerned, the actual situation is extremely serious, not to say tragic . . . laden with political consequences . . . considering that . . . you see, don't you see? . . . the aforesaid Février is hand in glove with the Minister of Interior and Justice . . . uh . . . uh . . . If I didn't have this wretched cold which unexpectedly ties me down upon a bed of pain, I should have gone at once to see our great old friend, Senator Aristhène, who also . . . by sufficient grace from the Almighty . . . has the ear of His Excellency the President of the Republic."

"Granted, Mayor Origène, gran-ted! But what the devil paralyzes your eloquent hand and prevents you from quickly dispatching to him a fully detailed apologia of our life, public as well as private?"

"That's exactly what I'm going to do . . . you see.

. . . But before I do, however, you must . . . don't you see? . . . uh . . . uh . . . speak to me *in vino veritas,* as it is so well expressed in that cursed Latin you love so much to quote . . . and which used to cause me all sorts of problems when I was in school. Bolster yourself with a few little glasses of this divine Barbancourt and tell me the truth, the whole truth, and nothing but the truth."

"Willingly, dear friend, willingly," said the Justice of the Peace, who was quite thirsty after this delicate conversation.

And he gulped down three full glasses, one after the other. Then, by way of rewarding the Mayor for his humanistic courtesy: *"Nunc est bibendum!"* he sighed, wittily patting his flat belly.

"Tell me, Justice Sèpe," asked the Mayor with the abstract bluntness of an inquisitor, "were you in bed with La Paloma when they came looking for you the night in question, to make your report on the profanation of the church?"

"No, Mayor Origène, three times no!" replied Septimus Morency. "I have never fornicated with the Messalina of the city."

"Then what was she doing in your house at that late hour? . . . uh . . . uh . . . She was whispering in your ear . . . was she . . . jealous neighborly gossip?"

The Justice of the Peace modestly lowered his eyes. "She was simply trying to seduce my incorruptible virtue of a lay anchorite," he said in a low voice with false contrition. "First she tried to force her way into my austere abode by the entrance portico, where she was knocking with the shattering impetuosity of a mad stevedore on a Bacchic spree. I cautiously opened one of the shutters of the diptych, and when I saw that all she had on was a nocturnal shift, I quickly closed the aforesaid shutter. Then the trollop, with the Caesarian determination of the Roman consul crossing the Rubicon and the forest agility of the wistitis, in the twinkling of an eye climbed up the avocado tree . . . or rather, as you have just pejoratively defined it with a grain of Attic salt: 'my feeder tree.' And she quickly jumped over the balcony railing and maliciously entered the secret intimacy of my bedroom, inviolate until then!"

"Wasn't she supposed . . . uh . . . uh . . . to be possessed by Mistress Erzilie?"

"Not at all, dear friend, not at all! That Hispanic female is a histrionic tragicomedienne. With respect to the possession, all I can deduce from that sordid and crude, albeit very fragrant, misadventure is that the infernal fire of original concupiscence was lustfully burning in the demented seat of her volcanic sexuality. And, this said, I conclude with the cold impartiality of the Solomonian jurists, in full knowledge of the causalities, for that hysterical vivandière, first of all, having enfolded me with serpentine litheness, was demoniacally crushing my solar plexus with the suggestive and inexorable weight of her everlasting breasts. It wasn't long before she communicated to me the fire that was eating at her incandescent innards. So I was on the verge of slipping when, by a providential act of charity from the Almighty, Sergeant Fortuné, in turn, came knocking at the entrance portico. . . ."

"And that is, my poor Septimus, what saved you from the disgrace . . . isn't it? . . . of betraying a friend . . . uh . . . uh . . . only that?"

"I had to contribute something too, dear friend, a

coefficient that is far from constituting a negligible quantity, for I could just as well have turned a deaf ear. Moreover, as I was freeing myself from her sinuous and persuasive embrace, the whore vigorously took hold of my genitals and threatened to crush them between the convincing vise of her shameless claws if I tried to escape. Whence the virulent discussion they are holding against your humble servant, instead of crediting him with it in the ledger of his exemplary virtue. . . . In short, anxious to free myself without imperiling the delicate, nay fragile, attributes of my virility, I dealt her, without warning, a lightning uppercut that sent her piteously sprawling to the floor in a decisive knock-down. Then I stoically escaped from the voluptuous temptation and converged toward the geometric locus where duty was calling me. . . . And so those are the authentic episodes of what you designate, not without jeering, 'the mysterious affair of the avocado tree.' Evil to him who thinks evil!"

"Concerning your adventure with La Paloma, I would agree. . . . But we still have to delabyrinth the foggy secret of your monthly escapades to the Frontier . . . uh . . . uh . . . don't we? . . . The town councilman Louis-Jean Février, as well as the driver of the Boar of the Mountain—who, it seems to me, are now in cahoots to ruin us both—will not run out of inventive and scandalous anecdotes about sexual orgies which, according to their shameless talk . . . uh . . . uh . . . you see . . . you are in the habit of perpetrating openly before the international riff-raff of the milieu!"

The Justice of the Peace, overwhelmed, did not have the strength to defend himself. Tears came to his eyes. Disturbed to see him in such disarray, Macdonald Origène got out of his "bed of pain" without a groan,

poured three fingers of rum in a large glass, and chari-
tably held it out to his friend.

"Drink, Sèpe, my friend," he said simply.

Then, afraid he might get a chill, he hurried back
into bed.

XVI

When he came out of his daze, Septimus Morency had
no trouble clearing himself of the accusations of debauchery made against him by Louis-Jean Février and
Rénélus Altidor. All he had to do was to bring out the
hygienic character of his trips to Port-au-Prince, by
confessing in manly fashion that, for all his being a
scrupulous Justice, he was still made of flesh, like everyone else. As far as the Frontier was concerned, being
careful about his respectability, he had never ventured
there. He certainly might have been seen in the neighborhood, when he went at night to see *la belle* Francine,
whose discreet tavern, frequented by honorable public
officials, was located on the rue Saint-Honoré, in the
third block of houses to the east of the aforesaid quarter
of perdition.

Where was the harm? Wasn't it in that modest establishment that seven or eight years before, introduced by
Senator Aristhène, he had met Macdonald Origène and
had made friends with him? Afterwards . . .

At this point, the Mayor of Boischandelle, who did
not at all want his wife to hear this much too "relevant"

part of the Justice's confession, was making desperate signs for him to lower his voice. But Septimus Morency was looking at the floor with a meditative and offended air, so that he did not see—or pretended not to see—this eloquent entreaty. Besides, he was going full tilt.

Afterwards, he continued in a baritone voice with the tranquil conscience of the just, didn't he and Mac used to meet at Francine's, always in the company of their great friend Jean Baptiste Napoléon Aristhène, and hadn't they shared with that respectable old man, recently condemned to widowhood by a decree of destiny, the free favors of the sweet, passionate tavernkeeper, who never refused a *belle* to distinguished customers?

"Justice Sèpe," solemnly said Macdonald Origène, anxious to cut short the compromising chatter, "why . . . uh . . . uh . . . didn't you ever marry?"

"I?" asked the Justice of the Peace, startled, as though the question had touched a painful spot.

He bowed his head and from lips contorted with bitterness came this laconic reply: "Alas!"

"Didn't you tell me that at the blessed time of your youth . . . uh . . . uh . . . didn't you? . . . that you were on the point of embarking upon legal matrimony?"

"Twice, Mayor Origène, twice I attempted to settle down!" corrected poor Septimus, honestly.

And he evoked sadly, but with his usual humor, a humiliating past in which he had been caught between man's cruelty and his own bad luck.

He made a first attempt in the noble city of Les Cayes, cradle of his family. The fiancée's trousseau was all ready and he had just furnished the modest house where they were to live after the wedding, when the intemperate Yankee who had forced Septimus to drink a whole bottle of rum with him, and had become his friend after that initial encounter, seduced the girl and made her his mistress.

The second attempt took place in Port-au-Prince, where he took refuge to hide his shame. This time, proudly offering his arm to the matron of honor, he was about to enter the church for the marriage ceremony with his bride when a cynical urchin came and stood squarely in front of him with hands on his hips and berated him in these terms: "Hey, Papa, are you getting married again?"

It was, they learned later from an item in the *Papyrus*, only a stupid prank staged by a practical joker from around there; but the parents of the bride-to-be did not take the thing lightly. Since he was from the province and they had not checked into his marital status, they foolishly believed he had fooled them. "The scoundrel was going to lead my daughter into bigamy," roared the father, raising his hands to heaven. "He was going criminally to soil her virginal purity!" So, despite his denials, the other members of the tribe fell upon him, Septimus, beat him black and blue, and left him all but lifeless on the parvis, while the bells were joyfully announcing to the entire parish of St. Anne the celebration of his mariage.

Macdonald Origène should understand, consequently, that since life had thus thwarted his "matrimonial endeavors," he became wary of that kind of enterprise, always fraught with risks, and as a tribute to the genetic instinct, he settled for the venal or free favors of professionals, who, at least in matters of love, had a perfected technique and a craftsman's taste for work well done.

But the Mayor of Boischandelle's curiosity was not satisfied.

"After the explicit item in the *Papyrus*," he said to the Justice of the Peace, "didn't the girl's parents make apologies . . . uh . . . uh . . . and offer you her hand again?"

"I should say not!" replied Septimus. "They headed straight to the other extreme of the polite direction required by the most rudimentary decency and they hastened to chain their passive offspring to the marital yoke of the very scoundrel who engineered the trick of the bigamy."

"Strange ending, dear friend . . . uh . . . uh . . . isn't it? . . . but also, such haste, such precipitation!"

"It is true that previously, in my superlative but justified resentment, I notified them by an intermediary that, having enjoyed the supreme favors of their little hypocrite without meeting any membranous resistance at the antechamber of the venereal sheath, I knew something about her 'virginal purity.' But the hilarious climax of the whole affair is that, by the admission of the little goose herself, the aforesaid scoundrel had cleared the way for me, with the astute expectation that once I discovered the breaking of the seal (whose permanence I had two days before digitally verified), I would scrap my matrimonial plans. The boor was gauging me by his petty yardstick of a tree-dwelling primate. But when it became abundantly clear that I was chivalrously determined not to create a scandal within the family circle of my intended by repudiating her for premarital infidelity, he found no recourse but to hurl his snotty bastard at me and hamstring me, like a *coup de Jarnac,* and accuse me, at the crucial and decisive

145

moment, of a legitimate paternity which could not have been attributable to me, even putatively, considering that celibate loneliness has always been my lot."

Septimus Morency shook his head and smiled stoically.

"The fact is that the hussy had a dowry of substantific dough, and before I entered the race, they had refused to put it into the apelike paws of the ignorant and unlicked anthropoid he is."

And with that, judging he had said enough on the subject, the Justice of the Peace got up to leave. But the Mayor still had some questions.

"Why then, Sèpe, my dear friend," he asked, lowering his voice (but not enough to prevent Madame Origène, who had a sharp ear, from hearing), "why then . . . to stop exposing your flank to the poisoned arrows of slander . . . uh . . . uh . . . don't you see? . . . all the more so because it would save you the trouble of those recurring trips to Port-au-Prince . . . and every day you could satisfy the urgent demands of the flesh . . . uh . . . uh . . . instead of ascetically limiting yourself to two or three embraces a month . . . you see . . . why then, I say, don't you take a mistress in the village of Boischandelle? . . . uh . . . uh . . . No one would take exception to it . . . the town councilman Louis-Jean Février least of all . . . he, who . . . don't you see? . . . openly keeps two concubines at the marketplace!"

"That's something to mull over, dear friend," said Septimus Morency evasively, for he was wary of any tie, even a casual one.

"It seems to me, Justice Sèpe," resumed Macdonald Origène, piqued by the lack of enthusiasm his suggestion inspired in the Justice of the Peace, "it seems to

146

me . . . isn't it so? . . . that the beauties of the town
don't strike your refined patrician fancy . . . uh . . .
uh . . . that you find them too rough . . . too rustic.
. . . If that's the case, why not import a girl from Port-
au-Prince? The passionate Francine, for example . . .
uh . . . uh . . . She could open a tavern on the
Grand-Rue . . . don't you see? . . . and the crowds of
tourists who visit the Pine Forest all year round, stopping in town after getting a tank full of gas, would at
last find a pleasant little place to have a cool drink.
What do you think of that, dear friend?"

"That you are certainly thinking like a municipal
official with vision who has a care for the good name of
the city he administers. But where, in all that, where
does our great friend Senator Aristhène come in? And
where, great God, would I find the parricidal strength
to take away from that venerable patriarch the consola-
tion of his old age, already shrouded in gloom by the
premature disappearance of the one with whom, for six
consecutive lustres, he knew the euphoric tenderness of
Hymen?"

The Mayor gave him the ghost of a compassionate
smile.

"I can see very well, Sèpe, my dear friend, that you
did not know the deceased when she was alive. She was a
mustached shrew with the walk of a Cossack . . . an
appetizing mulatto, it's true, but a whole head taller
than her husband . . . uh . . . uh . . . ferociously
jealous, on top of that . . . in a word, a veritable
tigress! Her death . . . you can imagine . . . far from
crushing our friend with grief . . . uh . . . uh . . .
was a deliverance. Just imagine that she would come
sometimes, bull's pizzle in hand, to get him in those
decent little night spots . . . you see . . . where, in

the company of pleasing, easy hostesses, he relaxed in his free time . . . with that lively good nature, always dignified, that you know him to have . . . from the burdensome duties of the Senate . . . uh . . . uh . . . and she would bring him back, hitting him all the way, to the infernal fold. As far as *la belle* Francine is concerned, don't worry about it, Justice Sèpe. She is only one of many protégées of Senator Aristhène . . . and she's pushing middle age . . . uh . . . uh . . . He wouldn't hold it against you . . . he gets blasé so quickly . . . you see . . . for taking that charming tavernkeeper out of the abundantly stocked circle he frequents. Besides, he's so accommodating, so generous . . . uh . . . uh . . . always ready to share a good find with his young friends!"

"Very strong, dear friend, ve-ry strong, but also very debatable," trumpeted the Justice of the Peace. "And what about my congenital impecuniosity, incurably irreversible because of my equally inborn integrity? You also know the Lacedaemonian frugality of my meager salary of a praetor everlastingly assigned to the highland bush. How could I, over and above the rent and grub, finance that coquette's insidious furbelows that are as indispensable to her as food and drink? Would you, by any chance, be disposed to sharing with me (for I am hardly exclusive), on the one hand, the favors of that long-haired brunette, and on the other, the onerous disbursements that our Babylonian arrangement, in all fairness, would necessitate?"

"Peace!" whispered the Mayor excitedly as he made roguish gestures of acquiescence. "Peace, Septimus, peace!"

It was too much for Madame Origène. She opened the bedroom door noisily, her face majestic, full of Olympian wrath, and advanced with dramatic deliberation toward the two stupefied accomplices.

"I always knew," she declared, looking them up and down, "that men in general are dirty pigs, always ready to jump on any female in sight. But I excluded both of you, as well as Senator Aristhène, thinking naïvely that you were exceptions. And now . . ."

At the end of her rope, for all the reminiscences of the gallant life had her in a flutter, she collapsed on the rug and sobbed despondently. Septimus Morency made the best of it and took French leave. But Macdonald Origène, with practiced eye, sized up the situation very quickly. He had seen many others . . . don't you see? . . . uh . . . uh . . .

Slowly, laboriously, he lifted the heavy Eudovia up on the conjugal bed and turned up her skirts. Far from needing any coaxing, she raised her powerful legs obediently to permit her libidinous mate to establish perfect contact, their respective bellies requiring this tiring posture. And without preliminary, he penetrated her.

Then, closing his eyes, he imagined intensely that it was in turn La Paloma and *la belle* Francine, instead of his worthy spouse, whom he was taking on his "bed of pain."

A belated offspring was conceived in this fraudulent embrace.

XVII

It was the evening before St. Claire's Day. Boischandelle, invaded by a seething crowd of pilgrims and revelers, had feverishly prepared to celebrate its patron saint's feast. Ceding to a request by Eudovia, whom he had not been able to pacify entirely, Macdonald Origène, with the assistance of his neighbors, had erected an altar on the porch of his home for the procession which was to take place the following morning; three of the village notables, because it was their turn, had done the same, while the others settled for decorating their houses with rugs, colored fabrics, and bouquets of roses. Chickens, turkeys, and even goats and pigs had been killed for the traditional feasting.

Near the marketplace, about a week before, there had been erected coconut palm arbors on both sides of the Grand-Rue, which became lively with noise at nightfall. By the flickering light of the smoky lampions, you could buy alcoholic beverages, cola-champagne, or—in an appetizing smell of hot fat—pork *grillot,* fried fish, beans and rice, chicken or dried cod fritters, popular foods, highly seasoned with hot pepper, served in wrapping paper and eaten casually and greedily with the fingers. But under other more spacious arbors people were playing dice, and some excited couples, hips swaying right and left, were vigorously dancing the *pignite* to the frenzied rhythm of the conical drums and the most licentious songs of the year.

A little to one side of the tumult of the crowd, in a little two-room house, which was formerly used as a warehouse by Jean-Baptiste Napoléon Aristhène when he speculated in coffee, *la belle* Francine had opened a tavern for the duration of the festivities. That night it was full of the local big shots who lingered there after taking a look around the grounds. The old Senator came as he did every night, accompanied by his two protégés, Macdonald Origène and Septimus Morency, as well as Deputy Pierre Legrand, a young cousin whom he had launched into politics but who was supposed to have had connections for some time with Louis-Jean Février.

Contrary to the spiteful talk of the gossips—who asserted that in the early morning hours, once the Deputy and other clients left, the honorable conscript father and his "associates," quite drunk by then, fornicated savagely with the hostess and the waitresses—*la belle* Francine's tavern had an irreproachable decorum, despite the heavy drinking done there. Madame Origène could attest to it, because Macdonald always came back to the conjugal hearth by early morning, full of impetuous desires that he appeased in her until sunrise.

The only reprehensible place—nevertheless frequented by Louis-Jean Février and his avowed partisans, among whom was the town councilman Théodore Adonis—was the hangar that Rénélus Altidor had leased on the marketplace for his crony from the Frontier, Féfé Duchemin, leader of the famous orchestra named "The Criminals."

This shady character, a hoodlum proud of his viciousness, who did not hide the fact that he was a spy for the Department of the Interior, arrived one fine morning, making a big racket with his musicians and a whole gang of prostitutes and pimps.

They had scarcely got off the Boar of the Mountain when they undressed outdoors, leaving on, depending on their sex, only their shorts or pants. Then, in a Dionysiac procession, the males holding a bottle of rum with one hand and with the other a female with bouncing breasts, they all headed in double time toward Bassin-Bleu, while the athletic Duchemin, with a Dominican girl astride on his shoulders, was wildly playing a cornet and the rest of the troop was singing loud enough to split the ears:

> My feet don't touch, ouaille-oh!
> My feet don't touch the ground, ouaille-oh!
> My feet don't touch, ouaille-oh!
> My feet don't touch the ground, ouaille-oh!
> Ouaille-oh! Ouaille-oh!
> Ouaille-oh! Ouaille-oh!
> How fast the siren Diamant walks, aïbobo!
> How fast the siren Diamant walks, aïbobo!
> How fast the siren Diamant walks, aïbobo!
> How fast the siren Diamant walks, aïbobo!
> My feet don't touch, ouaille-oh!
> My feet don't touch the ground. . . .

When they arrived at the cascade—ancient pilgrimage site where the black Virgin of Higüey, they say, appears every spring among the new leaves of an old palm tree—

that wild gang took off their shorts and pants, and still shouting their intrepid song, they copulated like animals in the basin hollowed out by the falls, routing the devout, who had come from all over the country as well as from the neighboring republic.

The Ambassador of the United States and his wife happened to be in the vicinity, and it is claimed that as seasoned tourists, each on his own filmed the scene with typical Anglo-Saxon determination, convinced that they were witnessing a fertility rite worthy of being recorded for the education of their friends and relatives, and especially for the briefing in Washington, D.C. of the diplomats assigned to Port-au-Prince.

Bellami had immediately been presented with detailed charges against Féfé Duchemin and his band; but the poor man knew whom he was up against and he remembered the reprimands and disgrace brought on him by the arrest of Dr. Karl Marx. So he left in a hurry "on an inspection tour" to Terre-Froide, where he often went to meet—in order to forget his marital woes—a young peasant girl with eyes like a startled dove, smelling of mint, fresh spring water, and pine resin.

The village notables were quite indignant. And since the Soldiers of St. Michael remained silent, held back by the same fear as the Lieutenant, all they could count on now was heaven to avenge them for the outrage against decency which victimized the commune—an outrage which, in their estimation, was close to sacrilege.

Everyone, including Rénélus Altidor himself, was offended.

"I'd like to know why, with utter disrespect for the Virgin and St. Claire, you've made this big scandal in Boischandelle," he had said afterwards to Féfé Duchemin, while the latter, his conscience clear, was tuning his guitar and looking preoccupied. "I'm very much afraid that's an obscenity for which you and your gang will pay very dear."

"Pay whom?" Féfé asked with a sarcastic smile. "The Good Lord, maybe?"

"If not the Good Lord, at least the authorities."

"The authorities! Don't you see, Rénélus, that you're like a newborn baby? What do you know about the politics of the government?"

"Not much, of course. But I'm sure it has nothing to do with your indecent behavior of this morning. You felt like having a *partouze;* well, you could have chosen another place where no one could see you. If necessary, I could have lent you my house, provided you closed all the doors. And besides, what was the reason for that naked pageant?"

"Do you know the instructions I was given?"

"I don't need to know them to realize that they didn't ask you and your gang to do what you did here and at Bassin-Bleu."

"They asked me to do something even stronger. . . . Anyway, Rénélus, you're here, you'll see."

"Something even stronger?" asked the bus driver, astounded. "You're not out of your mind, no?"

"I can't tell you about it right now, but when the time comes I'll tell you all about it because I need your help."

"To help you create another scandal? I won't go along."

"You'll go along, dear Rénélus, you'll go along," Féfé said, plucking lightly at his guitar. "In high places, where they appreciate your bold courage, they advised me to ask you to give me a hand, for they haven't forgotten that during the American occupation you

154

used to have a great time beating up the drunken Marines who attacked Haitians in the street or in the cafés of the Frontier. If you lend me a hand, you'll get your reward; if not, you'll get in trouble. Understand? On the slightest pretext . . . and it's the easiest thing in the world to find one . . . they could revoke your driving license. Besides, you know how they made a *submarine* out of me. First, they threw me in jail for some trifling stupidities, and they did it so often I began to think the state was just doing it for kicks. Then one fine day they made me an offer to join the *detectives*. They gave me a revolver. And since then I sell my cocaine with a quiet heart, as though it's powdered sugar. I don't need to say more than that. . . ."

Hence, that evening, with complete impunity, Féfé Duchemin's dance was in full swing. And pooh-poohing the general disapproval of the notables, the gilded youth of Boischandelle were having a good time to the relentless hip-swaying beat of a vodou dance, arranged for the occasion in a vigorous *haler-brouette:*

Ahiman Ibo Lélé,
Lélé, Lélé, Lélé,
Ahiman Ibo Lélé,
You step on my toes,
You ask my pardon.
Will your pardon cure me?
Will your pardon cure me?
Will your pardon cure me?
Ahiman Ibo Lélé,
Lélé, Lélé, Lélé,
Ahiman Ibo Lélé,
You step on my toes,
You ask my pardon.

Will your pardon cure me?
Will your pardon cure me?
Will your pardon cure me?
Will your pardon . . .

About midnight a squall, coming in furtively, swooped down on the town with extraordinary violence, just at the moment when Féfé Duchemin, doing his utmost to be as guttural as an Afro-Cuban tenor, was singing his latest composition, dedicated to the "revered mentor of the Haitian nation":

President Eliacin,
It's you the people love.
President Eliacin,
It's you the people love.
You can stay ten years [in power],
You can stay twenty years,
You can stay thirty years,
That's no problem, Papa.
It's you the people love. . . .

The hangar, located to the south of the marketplace, was exposed. When the first gust gripped it, it resisted, groaning in all its beams, while the arbors along the Grand-Rue, being more fragile, were carried off like so much straw; but the second time it hit, the storm easily ripped off the roof.

A torrential rain followed.

The Ambassador of the United States and his wife, who were planning to drive down to Port-au-Prince before daybreak, were obliged to run for shelter in the tavern of *la belle* Francine, who thought it best to invite them to the table of honor, which was occupied of course by Jean-Baptiste Napoléon Aristhène and his friends.

Now, since he had missed the good opportunity that La Paloma had offered him, Septimus Morency, haunted by lustful visions that kept him from sleeping, took his liquor badly and was becoming embittered. At the moment he was drunk and ultra-nationalist—his first fiancée, we recall, was seduced by an American—so he saw red.

"Monsieur the Ambassador of Yankeeland, get the hell out of here, and on the double," he said in a hoarse voice, totally oblivious of courtesy and even of his "fine speech."

But Senator Aristhène, affable old man, well versed in the compromises of diplomacy, motioned to *la belle* Francine. She whispered a few enticing words in the Justice's ear and put her arm around his waist. He got up immediately, believing it was a sincere invitation, and took leave of his companions. She led him to the lean-to that served as her bedroom, whence she emerged almost instantly, double-locking the door.

XVIII

Realizing he had been tricked like a child, Septimus Morency became violently angry. He was on the point of wrecking the room when his eyes fell upon a bottle of rum that the tavernkeeper had set on the bedside table before she slipped out. He took hold of it with a spirit of vengeance. They thought he was drunk; well, he'd show them! He drank a fourth of it down, straight from the bottle. And without bothering to take off his shoes, he stretched out on the bed, his brain in a complete black-out.

The flame of the lamp was flickering for lack of kerosene; soon it went out. But the Justice of the Peace could not fall asleep. It seemed to him that by turns his head and feet rose to the ceiling and fell back down again in an agonizing seesaw movement. That prodigy, which he soon took for real, lasted a whole eternity. Then the bed began whirling around like a phonograph record with accelerating speed, as cold sweat streamed out of his pores. Finally, he came to the gates of Paradise and heard the choir of angels extolling the everlasting glory of the Almighty in the heavenly vineyards. Could

I be deceased? he wondered, hoping that death had borne him away from the miseries of this insane world. It was nothing of the sort. It was only *la belle* Francine, who, now that the shower was over and her clients had left, was bringing in another lamp, as she sang:

> Ogou works, oh! Ogou does not eat!
> Ogou works, oh! Ogou does not eat!
> All he earns he gives to beautiful women.
> Last night he went to bed without supper!

She undressed, casually. And proceeding methodically, she took off the jacket, shoes, then the trousers of her old friend, and lay down beside him with the firm intention of making amends to him for his diplomatic imprisonment—for, although she was not in love with him, she did have a penchant for him that bordered on tenderness and came from the maternal instinct. He seemed so defenseless in the battle of life, so childish with his "fine speech," that, since she could not take him in her arms and cuddle him like a baby, she was always happy to consent, in an almost incestuous way, to his hygienic "embraces," whose vigor and precision, none the less, showed perfect virility.

Suddenly Septimus Morency's insides quickened with a turbulent feeling that sexual desire had in no way provoked. His throat tightened. He sat up quickly, looked for the chamber pot, found it, and threw up in it copiously while his kind hostess, full of solicitude, held his temples. . . .

About four o'clock, the bells of St. Claire were summoning the faithful to the first Mass. The Justice of the Peace, who was in the habit of going on Sundays and holy days of obligation, wanted to dress to go to church, but his strength failed him. The tavernkeeper went to

159

pick a lemon in the courtyard, cut it, and rubbed the juice on his temples and behind his ears. She also made him take two aspirins with milk. Then she gave him a bottle of smelling salts and told him to inhale them on the way.

So it happened that Septimus Morency, his legs still quite weak, was able to go without staggering to meet his fate. He had just entered the church when Féfé Duchemin's gang, bolstered by Rénélus Altidor and the *boeuf-chaîne* Ciceron, began to fire on the holy images. The result was an indescribable panic in the crash of overturned chairs, as women and children, knocked down by men rushing toward the exit, cried out in despair.

We cannot say how the Justice of the Peace found the strength to push his way to the niche where St. Claire stood. The fact is that he perched on a seat and protected the statue with his body, without realizing that the attackers could just as well aim at him. A bullet hit him under the left shoulder blade and, piercing the pleura, passed only a millimeter from his heart. He collapsed on the stone floor of the transept, and as if to emphasize the futility of his gesture, at that very moment a blasphemous missile knocked the head off the statue of the patron saint of Boischandelle.

For his part, Father Le Bellec at first tried to continue celebrating the Mass as though nothing had happened, believing he could intimidate the enemy by his courage, but since the choir boys had fled, he was obliged to leave. When the disorder was over and he went back into the church to see the damage, he was painfully surprised to find the Justice of the Peace lying like a corpse close to the head of St. Claire. Trembling with emotion, he felt the pulse, and sighed with relief to find the

Justice still alive. But since Septimus had scarcely bled and was stretched out on his back, it did not occur to the young priest that he might be wounded. Convinced that it was merely a loss of consciousness caused by fear, he tried to bring him to with the help of the sacristan.

Their efforts succeeded only in provoking the hemorrhage which the Justice's immobility had held in check; then they understood the real cause of his fainting. Although he was horrified at the thought that there had been an attempt on the life of one of the faithful during the holy sacrifice of the Mass (a circumstance which certainly aggravated the profanation of the church), Father Le Bellec lost no time in vain maledictions. He dispatched the sacristan to the dispensary to get the help of Dr. Lauriston, the doctor on probation who had just been assigned to the commune of Boischandelle. . . .

The procession was held, just the same. Despite its mutilation, the statue of the saint was carried, as usual, by four notables. And to the great astonishment of the people of Boischandelle, who wept with compassion, Macdonald Origène marched in front of the bearers, with the head of the patron saint in his hands.

Meantime, their mission accomplished with all the brutality ordered "in high places," Féfé Duchemin and his gang, accompanied by the merry prostitutes of the Frontier, piled into the Boar of the Mountain. During the whole trip—except for Rénélus Altidor, who, being a careful driver, wanted to "keep his eyes clear"—they stuffed themselves with sandwiches and washed them down with beer or rum, shouting obscene songs the while—a veritable *barbaco!* They were already far away when the townspeople began to whisper that they were the ones who had opened fire in the church, but since they had not been caught in the act (for they had been

careful to fan out into the dark corners of the church),
no one dared, out of fear of reprisal, to make an open
accusation. Therefore, when the government later ordered an investigation as a matter of form, no one
brought charges against them. . . .

When he opened his eyes, Septimus Morency, who
still thought he was at the gates of heaven, listening to
the angelic choir, was very surprised to find himself
at the dispensary and to learn that he was seriously
wounded. Dr. Lauriston gave him a brief report of all
he knew about his adventure, but dwelt a long time on
the "instigators of the disorder." In his opinion, those
who had struck the blow, so that they could fish in
troubled waters, were conspirators, enemies of the Chief
of State and of the Catholic priests as well. And he had
every reason to suspect that the Protestants and the
vodou believers were in cahoots to set the fire of civil
war in the four corners of the country.

But the Justice of the Peace was preoccupied with
another question. He failed to grasp for what reason the
agents of the Secretary of State for the Interior had fired
on him, "a fearless representative of the law and, what is
more, a well-known supporter of the present regime"!
Had they been ordered to kill him? But if so, to what
end? He searched a long time, then he saw a glimmer of
light. He recalled that, as he was rushing toward the
statue of the saint, he caught a glimpse of the jealous
lover of La Paloma, furtively sneaking inside a confes-
sional with something hidden under his jacket that
could well be . . . that could only be a weapon . . . a
pistol, obviously!

"I am sure," confided Septimus to Dr. Lauriston,
"that it is the man named Rénélus who upon my person
opened fire."

"Shh!" said the doctor. "You mustn't talk at all, for the slightest effort could be fatal. . . ."

About noon an ambulance came for the Justice of the Peace and took him to the General Hospital in Port-au-Prince.

Dr. Lauriston had simply dressed his wound and given him an anti-tetanus shot. He refrained from extracting the bullet, which, after piercing Septimus's thorax, had lodged under the skin near the left breast. A slight incision would have been enough to remove it, but since there was no urgency and no equipment at the dispensary for surgical treatment, the young practitioner, considering the political climate, thought it prudent to shift onto the authorities of the Faculty a responsibility that could have consequences for his future.

It was a wise decision and he saw this clearly afterwards. For the President of the Republic was very annoyed at the disturbing incident that had bloodied the police operation at Boischandelle. He sent his private doctor to the hospital immediately after the arrival of the wounded man, to report on his condition. And the information service of the Department of the Interior did not fail to advise the press. It even took the trouble to have its communiqué read several times over the radio. But the Chief's troubles were not alleviated for all that. The Archbishop of Port-au-Prince, in a pastoral letter of elevated tone though in cryptic words, hinted at the odious, grotesque behavior of the government agents, but openly stated his feeling about the profanation of the churches in general. Consequently, the "revered mentor of the Haitian nation" went in person to the Justice of the Peace's bedside to comfort him like a good paterfamilias and, especially, to shut him up. Septimus Morency was, in short, only an accidental victim of the reaction—brutal, to be sure, but legitimate—of the patriots concerned regarding the subversive schemes of the Breton clergy.

Revolted by such behavior, which seemed to him gross and ridiculous to say the least, Macdonald Origène considered resigning. It took the intelligent intervention of Estinval Civilhomme, now more worried than ever about his son-in-law's political future, to dissuade him from doing it; but he went along reluctantly with the old man's practical reasoning. And toward the end of the discussion, things all but fell apart.

"I absolutely share your indignation, son," Estinval said before he left. "You know which side I'm on. Only, you see, in a situation like this, you always have to add some water to your wine. Because if you want to succeed . . ."

"Do you take me, by chance, for a vulgar climber . . . uh . . . uh . . . do you? . . . for a shameless pusher?"

"That's not what I meant, son. But you must understand . . ."

"No, monsieur, no!" said the Mayor, getting up to put an end to the discussion. "I don't want to understand."

Nevertheless, he followed his father-in-law's advice.

As for Septimus Morency, he recovered rather quickly. At the end of a week he left the hospital. And soon, although he was offended by the hypocritical solicitude the President of the Republic had shown him after his quixotic adventure, which he had taken as "an insult at my honor cast" (in other words, at his intelligence), he resumed his duties as Justice of the Peace in a spirit of complete resignation; he had to eat.

At least, he still thought so.

And Boischandelle, trying to forget the deplorable events of which it had been the scene, little by little slipped back into the slow rhythm of provincial life. Rénélus Altidor, after a long absence which he attributed to an acute attack of malaria, reappeared at the steering wheel of the Boar of the Mountain, which the *boeuf-chaîne* Ciceron, ever loyal to his master, had just freshly painted. He was welcomed like a bird of ill omen, but he was not harassed. And Septimus Morency, whom he went to see as soon as he arrived, began to doubt that it was he who had made the attempt on his life.

XIX

Alcius was wasting away.

Since Josaphat Joseph forbade Hortense to frequent the Pentecostalist church, he had been able to talk to her only furtively and on very rare occasions. This situation had become intolerable to him in the long run, and consequently one day, all other solutions seeming impossible, he proposed that she elope with him. She refused, being an honest girl who feared God, her father, and what people would say.

It was then that he began to lose weight.

Convinced that her godson was homesick, Madame Origène sent him to his parents at Trou-Sec, to spend some time there. After a month the poor boy, full of frustrated longing, came back more sickly than before he left, his head bowed down, his eyes sunken in their sockets, and his face showing extreme despair.

The Mayor's wife was so distressed she called Dr. Lauriston for a consultation. And the young doctor, after a careful examination that revealed nothing alarming, said to Madame Origène with a mischievous smile: "They are so precocious around here, I wonder if he hasn't been doing too much chasing after the willing girls of the town."

Then, thinking of La Paloma (for it pleased him to believe in the attempted rape, which he considered heroic because her husband was a military man), he added: "A big strapping fellow like him!"

Madame Origène protested that her godson was innocent. On Sunday, his day off, he never went anywhere except to Pastor Bienaimé's. So that, insofar as his sexual life might have a bearing on his present state, she thought that continence rather than debauchery could be the cause of his wasting away. But she doubted that chastity could produce such an effect, because, to her knowledge, it had never debilitated the Catholic priests. They had to look elsewhere for the cause of his illness.

"In that case," said Dr. Lauriston, doing his best to keep a straight face, "first thing tomorrow morning send the boy to me at the dispensary for a blood test. He should also bring me a stool sample, for he may well have intestinal worms . . . or something else. . . . Anyway, I find his abdomen a little swollen."

The analysis of the feces showed that Alcius's abdomen harbored quantities of helminths. But since he must have been host to them since early infancy, one might well wonder if these parasites alone were responsible for his rapid loss of weight and especially for that lugubrious look, that deathly pale color, which made him scarcely recognizable. The partisans of the town councilman Louis-Jean Février chose to attribute his illness to a supernatural cause, an altogether ignominious one.

It happened that, during Alcius's stay in his native village, one of his uncles on his mother's side, who had the same given name as he, died suddenly. Since the age of puberty, so they said, the deceased, chosen by a beneficent *loa*, had carried out in this arid and desolate region the ritual function of deflowerer of dead virgins, and consequently was stricken by impotence with living women. The belief behind this macabre custom was that maidens could not appear before the Good Lord if they were buried intact, because the infernal spirits, fond of virginity, would not miss the chance to defile them in their tomb. That superstitious practice, which, it was said, had been quite widespread among the peasantry, was no longer complied with except by the women who bathed corpses, who worked simply, without ritual, with their finger. But, according to hearsay, only the people of Trou-Sec and environs had retained the primitive tradition.

Haiti is a land fertile in myths; it produces new ones every blessed day. And the credulity of the peasants, like that of the Breton priests, is infinite. Boss Février's partisans had a good chance to spread the rumor that, at the death of the necrophile uncle, the beneficent *loa* whose *horse* he was chose Alcius to replace him—whence the despair that consumed the young man. And naturally the whole blame fell on Madame Origène, that pillar of the Church who had prevented him from being converted to the Pentecostalist religion, the only hope within his reach, for only Pastor Bienaimé, thanks to his thorough knowledge of vodou, could have saved him from the terrible slavery which he knew threatened him.

Until then it was only a matter of gossip that people listened to because they liked scandal and especially because it was the off-season and no one had anything important to do. But one evening, after a wide search led by her father, in a dense wood not far from Bassin-

Bleu, where she had gone for water, they found the body of Hortense. She had been strangled. And as her skirt was raised up to her navel, they could see, high up on her thighs, spots of blood showing she had been raped. The partisans of Louis-Jean Février—Josaphat in the lead—hastened to accuse Alcius of the crime, claiming that he was madly in love with the girl and that, according to the rumors, he could never have possessed her unless she was dead.

Madame Origène did not lose her head for a moment. She was able to confirm that at the time of the murder (which, according to Dr. Lauriston, had taken place about two o'clock, shortly after neighbors had seen the victim at the falls) Alcius was tending the shop while she went to see a sick friend and from there went to church for confession. She produced some ten customers who testified that in her absence they had been served by her godson. And as it happens that grotesque incidents are often linked with tragedies, several immoral girls, envious of La Paloma's reputation, declared that it was Alcius who had "shown them about life" and that, after he got back from Trou-Sec, he had many times given them irrefutable proof of his manhood. One of them, visibly pregnant, swore on the head of her unborn child that he was its father.

The Justice of the Peace put all these declarations on record in his official report. But so great was the indignation of most of the local inhabitants that Septimus Morency, despite his own conviction of the young man's innocence, gave orders for his arrest, to save him from the fury of Josaphat Joseph's friends, and sent him under safe escort to Port-au-Prince. The following day he took the trouble of going to the Public Prosecutor's office in the capital to give an oral account of the facts which proved, in his opinion, the falseness of the accusation made against Alcius. There he learned that the poor boy had been delirious since his arrival and that, to be sure he was not feigning madness, he was taken to Pont-Beudet for a psychiatric examination.

Septimus spent the night at the tavern on the rue Saint-Honoré and slept in *la belle* Francine's arms without suspecting that it was the last time. The next day, informed that Alcius was committed to the insane asylum, he took the Boar of the Mountain back to Boischandelle. The bus was caught en route by a torrential rain, and despite Rénélus Altidor's precautions, it skidded, once again, at the curve of Montjoli. The passengers had to get off so the bus could be put back on the road and the shower soaked them to the bone.

Sèpe, not fully recovered from his wound, got home with a stitch in his side and a high fever. Dr. Lauriston, whom he called that evening, diagnosed it as pleurisy. Rushed to the hospital as an emergency case, he more or less recovered, after hovering several days between life and death. But scarcely three weeks had elapsed since his return to Boischandelle when it became clear that the Justice of the Peace was stricken by tuberculosis. Discouraged, having also lost the will to live, he asked to be retired, and his request was promptly granted.

It was about this time that people began to suspect that Rénélus Altidor, who was already regarded by some as the one who had fired at Septimus Morency, might be the murderer of Hortense Joseph. Shortly before the time of the crime, some peasants had seen him prowling around the vicinity where the body of the girl had been found. At the hearing held by the Justice of the Peace they had not given evidence against him because they were loath, as are all our country people, to be witnesses in a court; but now that they thought it was a dead issue, they were beginning to talk—in whispers, however, and not without reticence. Warned by one of his friends, Rénélus judged he would do well to clear out.

Under cover of night he piled all his belongings into the Boar of the Mountain, picked up La Paloma on the way—who for some time had expressed the desire to see her home town—and fled with her to the neighboring republic, without as much as a goodbye to the *boeuf-chaîne* Ciceron. Following this scandal, which made him the general laughing stock, Lieutenant Bellami requested and immediately obtained a transfer. To console himself, he took to his new post the young peasant girl from Terre-Froide whom he had seduced not so long before, to serve as maid of all work and to attenuate the pain his wife's misconduct caused him. Of course she would lose the fresh country smell of her native soil, but she would still have, as she did after he initiated her, those eyes of a frightened dove which attracted him at first glance, and she was as passionate as Dulce María, a quality he greatly appreciated.

Charles-Oscar had, it seemed, the vocation for cuckoldship.

But Madame Origène's rancor was tenacious. She did not forget that if Alcius had sunk into insanity, it was due mainly to the persecutions with which Rénélus Altidor had overwhelmed him, and she kept reminding her husband of it until he was quite upset. She was not mollified until, upon the insistence of poor Mac, Senator Aristhène went to see the proper authorities, and on the basis of public rumor accusing the bus driver of the rape and murder of Hortense, he pressed them to start proceedings for his extradition. They grudgingly promised to take action, and the fugitive was not bothered.

Soon after, he was seen again at the Frontier, where La Paloma had just opened a *dancing* under his protection, the Bar des Criminels, which Féfé Duchemin's band enlivened on weekends. Disgusted with the politics of the Chief of State, the Mayor of Boischandelle resigned "for reasons of health" and was replaced, of course, by the town councilman Louis-Jean Février. Madame Origène almost had a miscarriage, but life had other surprises in store for her.

About the middle of October, when the crusade of the *Rejetés,* routed by the drastic action of the secret police, was becoming only a painful memory, there was already talk of a reconciliation between the Church and the government. The Chief, it was said, had decided to consecrate the Republic of Haiti to Our Lady of Perpetual Help, for whom he had, it seemed, a very special devotion. He had informed the Archbishop of Port-au-Prince about it, who had no choice but to agree.

Finally, the news became official. Estinval, triumphant, went to see his son-in-law.

"I told you, son, that it was only a little family squabble and that the thing to do was to keep out of it so you wouldn't be an embarrassing witness when the reconciliation came. If you had listened to me, you'd still be Mayor of Boischandelle, and who knows how far you could have gone with the support of the good fathers?"

Mac, silencing his regrets and with greater dignity than ever, interrupted his speech. "Have I ever given you to understand . . . uh . . . uh . . . have I? . . . that I could be party to compromises and palinodes?" he asked, walking toward the door.

And without taking leave of his father-in-law, oblivious of the fact that it was the old man who had assured his reelection in the past, he went with slow and majestic step to Septimus Morency's house.

Knowing that his friend had galloping tuberculosis and his days were numbered, he went to see him every day and lavished all kinds of attention on him, like a sister of charity. At the onset of his illness, Macdonald Origène had offered to pay for treatment at the St.-Gérard Sanatorium. But honest Septimus—who had lost his taste not only for life but for "fine speech," his sweet folly—had stoically answered: "Since I must die, dear friend, the sooner the better."

XX

On a blond December morning, smelling of amber and orange peel and blessed by a sky of washed azure streaked with white, light as a morning glory, His Excellency the Archbishop of Port-au-Prince, assisted by his suffragens, was celebrating under the portico of the National Palace the pontifical Mass to mark the consecration of the country to Our Lady of Perpetual Help.

During the course of the edifying retreat preceding the event, the bishops, one after the other, condemned from the pulpit of the cathedral—in an allusive way, of course, but in terms clear enough to be understood by the faithful—the brutal reaction of the government to the so-called anti-superstition campaign, which the Chief, not without some reason, considered subversive.

Consequently, peace did not reign in the hearts of the people. And, far from effecting a reconciliation, as the hope had been, the ceremony that was unfolding gave everyone the painful impression of a mystification of which the Church of Haiti was the consenting victim.

To top it all, the President of the Republic, kneeling

close to the microphones and surrounded by his wife, children, and high government officials, was making a spectacle of himself for the crowd assembled on the lawn around the Palace and the Place L'Ouverture. And while his inane, thundering voice drowned out all the others, he made throaty effects as he recited the litanies of the Virgin:

O Mother of Perpetual Help, my heart overflows with confidence in thee, deign to hear me and answer my plea. . . .

The Second Lieutenant who replaced Bellami at Boischandelle—a young bourgeois from the capital, fresh from military school, as keen about popular music as he was interested in his advancement—had a radio. For this occasion he had installed a loudspeaker at the gable of the house which his predecessor passed on to him. So Septimus Morency and Macdonald Origène, already filled with the bitterness that lost illusions always leave in sensitive hearts, could get their fill of the heavy, droning diction of the "revered mentor of the Haitian nation":

O Mother of Perpetual Help, I love to come and pray at the foot of thy miraculous image. Always it awakens in my soul the most fervent confidence. In thine arms I see Jesus, my Savior and my God. . . .

Toward the end of the third part of the litanies, far from becoming hoarse with fatigue, the voice of the "spiritual, nay consubstantial son of the sublime mother of the Gracchi" became warmer, louder, belching with the brutal sounds of a slide trombone:

O Mother of Perpetual Help, thy blessed image eloquently reminds me of thy greatness. I see inscribed in it thy glorious title of Mother of God . . .

Septimus Morency, who, like the Knight of la Mancha, had regained his lucidity before crossing the threshold to life everlasting, said to his friend with a faint smile:

"After all, Mayor Origène, it is Boileau, yes, who was right:

All men are fools; and in their foolishness
They strive and differ only more or less.

He died discreetly in the night, tired of being an embarrassing witness.

GLOSSARY

The spelling *vodou* in this translation has been retained from the original French text in order to avoid confusion with *voodoo* or *hoodoo,* which refers in the United States to "exotic rites and magical practices." To quote the late Professor Melville J. Herskovits (in Funk & Wagnalls *Standard Dictionary of Folklore,* Volume II, p. 1172) : "The American word *hoodoo* is used in the southern United States to signify an evil force and, as used in the term *hoodoo man,* means practitioner of magic. The common use of the word *voodoo* to designate any New World African-derived Negro rite, found in popular and travel literature, is obviously incorrect."

asson: sacrificial rattle made from a gourd decorated with glass beads and snake vertebrae strung on a net

baka: dwarf *devil;* see *devil*

boccor: sorcerer

bush-priest: former sacristan who recites the Catholic prayers at the beginning of the *services* and baptizes the drums and other ritual objects *cabicha:* napping (in an armchair) ; comes from the Spanish *cabezada,* nodding of the head

devil: ogre, malevolent divinity

dévotions: militant Catholics

gangan: leaf doctor

grillot: crisply cooked small pieces of pork

guédé: spirit of death

habitation: country property, plantation

hogan: iron bell struck with a metallic stick

horse: person possessed by a vodou divinity

houmfor: vodou temple

houngan: vodou priest

hounsis: men and women initiates—the *bossales* have undergone the first stage of initiation, and the *canzos* the second stage; but it is generally women who sing and dance during the *services;* see *service*

je-renonce: devil

lan-mitan: the person who stands in the middle; i.e., the *houngan*

loa: vodou divinity; synonyms *mystère,* angel, saint

marassas: divine twins

mystère: see *loa*

peristyle: dance ring of beaten earth, covered with palm thatch or corrugated tin; attached to the *houmfor,* it is open on three sides

pitites-caille: literally, children-of-the-house; members of a vodou confraternity

placé, to be: to live in concubinage.

poteau-mitan: post located in the center of the *peristyle* and through which the *mystères* are supposed to come down from the sky

reine-chanterelle: choir leader, always a woman

Rejeté: a person who has rejected or renounced vodou

resté-avec: child or adolescent placed as a servant by his
     parents; receives no wages, but is housed, clothed,
     and fed by his masters; used pejoratively
service: vodou ceremony
tonnelle: arbor
zombi: person reduced to slavery by a sorcerer who, for
     that purpose, took the soul out of the body